Light Transports

Intercity

Editor: Steve Dearden

route

First Published by Route
PO Box 167, Pontefract, WF8 4WW
e-mail: info@route-online.com
web: www.route-online.com

ISBN: 1 901927 31 8

Editor:
Steve Dearden

Thanks to:
Emma Smith, Isabel Galan, Ian Daley
GNER, Network Rail, Midland Mainline
and First TransPennine Express

Cover Design
Steve Dearden and Andy Campbell

Printed by Bookmarque, Croydon

A catalogue for this book is
available from the British Library

Route is an imprint of ID Publishing
www.id-publishing.com

This book was possible thanks to support from
Illuminate. Illuminate is supported by the Millennium
Commission, Arts Council England, The National Lottery,
Yorkshire Culture, Yorkshire Forward, Bradford Metropolitan
District Council

Stories

Introduction

Welcome to Light Transports, reads to get you from A to B via somewhere else, each lasting a journey between cities.

On the surface these four pieces couldn't be more different – a Guyanese love story, a young German soldier's experience in occupied Czechoslovakia, an entertaining romp of international criminality and magical spells in rural France, and a woman who wants to disappear. What unites them is movement, across frontiers, through roles and identities, into other people's spaces.

Mark McWatt is a Guyanese Commonwealth Prize winner published by Peepal Tree Press in Leeds. Storm Jameson is one of Yorkshire's greatest writers who we should be lauding along with the usual suspects. The novelist Patricia Duncker, Professor of Creative Writing at the University of East Anglia, is involved in the region's programme for developing young writers. Novelist and critic Aritha van Herk has worked in the region as Yorkshire Arts International Writer in Residence, she lives in Calgary, Alberta and Penguin Canada recently had her write the history of the province.

These stories are locally grown or locally sourced – you can get in touch with the vibrant writing and reading going on in the Yorkshire region by visiting www.light-transports.net where there is much more on the writers in this book as well as links to the people who publish new writing and put on events in the region.

Steve Dearden

The Last Night
Storm Jameson

1

When I was a child I lived of course in our farm in Ruge, in East Prussia. The farmhouse had been built by my great-great-grandfather in the dip in the ground between two birch woods. The lake, our lake, was beyond the nearer wood. In front of the house the plain, its fields, woods, other lakes, the river, was all day long in full light, even when a shadow, the shadow of the birches, covered the house.

My grandfather, my mother – his daughter-in-law – and I, lived in the house with the house servants. The others slept in the low building that formed one side of the courtyard. Slept, I say, because for a long time I supposed that even their children were outside at work always. And this, at least when I was a child, was nearly true. Then my father died – in 1926, of the effects of his war wounds: he was a volunteer in the first war against England – and under the gentler rule of my grandfather there was more gaiety, the feeling that we were almost a family. The truth is that in our family a severe Reichel is always followed by a sensitive and less effective one: my grandfather would never, as did my father, have risked buying land in the bad years, nor driven his labourers to their limit to make the risk good. As for me, his son, I am neither hard, nor assured, nor sound. All the same, I am a Reichel, and when I look in the glass I see any Reichel – the sunken eyes, face hollowed under strong cheekbones, long mouth.

My mother and my grandfather are the same sort. I grew up between them like the grass between two birches, a little too fine. Not that they were soft with me – neither of them is soft. But there was a sympathy between us which made a closed family circle, and what is closed from the world never masters it. I had on my bed-table a photograph of my father in his lieutenant's uniform. It reproached me with my happiness. Since I was so young when he died, this photograph was my father. I cannot call up any other image of him. If now and then I think I remember a living man, the memory easily escapes and fades, shrinks, into the dry image on paper. Once I questioned my grandfather about his son: what was he like? was he very brave, a hero? After a minute my grandfather said quietly: 'He was a farmer turned good soldier.'

When I was four years old a stallion broke loose from the groom leading it. I was in the path of its brute flight, it only put a foot on me in rushing past, but my leg was fractured in three places, and for all the Berlin surgeon my grandfather fetched, I was lamed. I drag one foot, the right, as I walk. It was because of this that I lived quietly at home; I was not able to serve the Leader except by preparing to manage the farm well, grow more food, and, in time, marry and have children. I learned to ride. In spite of all, I became something of a jockey and believed I understood horses. It grieved me when I was older to know that my grandfather had had the stallion shot. My father would not have done it.

I was barely sixteen when England attacked Germany for the second time – this time through Poland. Because I could not look forward to being a soldier, I did what I could to live a life worthy of the war. I slept outside. In winter a piece of my skin froze to the rug I was using as a pillow and tore off when I moved. The pain heartened me. My grandfather – it is only now that I overhear the irony in his voice – said, 'A soldier doesn't run unnecessary risks.' He ordered me to wear a helmet my mother knitted, protecting all but my eyes.

After four years, the miracle. I was called up. When the order came I was alone in the house. I kneeled in front of the photograph and thanked the Leader for his mercy to me, his poor lame one. 'You will see,' I told him, 'that I am not a weakling.' I heard my mother in her room and went down. In my happiness, I had expected her to show pride; and I was disappointed when she said, staring at me, 'I thought you would be left to us.' With my grandfather, she was all the love, all the gentleness, all the warmth of my life – and I saw at the time only a door opening and myself running through it into the world. I was not more selfish than other children. It is even right that children turn their backs on a mother, a grandfather. You can see, in other countries, in France, for example, how love of the past destroys a people. Looking at my mother when she lit the lamp, I saw for the first time the lines, scored downward, on her fine skin.

All my grandfather said was, 'It will be summer before you are trained.'

I thought so myself, and I began to be afraid that during the weeks or months of training some officer would say, 'This lame fellow is no good....' A week after I reached Berlin I was in a train going east. I had been given a uniform, taught how to use a sub-machine-gun, and had shown that I could use a rifle. I saw nothing of Berlin – we were taken in a sort of horse-box to the station – and had no chance to see how much of it the barbarians had destroyed.

In the train I realised what I owed to living at Ruge. The other young men in the carriage were all, like me, what, the first day he saw us, our machine-gun instructor called 'defective parts'. One of us was almost blind, another had lost two fingers of his left hand, a third coughed until we all wearied of him. But where I was strong and perfectly healthy, nothing wrong except my dragging foot, these others were underfed, sickly, frightened. I became a little friendly with the half-blind boy. From what he said I thought that they had been living on the rations allowed to the very old and the stateless. It is just – the Leader needs soldiers and tireless workers. But then my happiness had been unjust... It means, I thought, that fate has an eye on me. My body was light and bursting with joy – the same feeling precisely as the cherry trees at Ruge gave me each spring. Afterwards I only felt hungry like the others. We had been given four biscuits, dry and quite tasteless, and the journey to Prague took ten hours. Before we crossed into the Protectorate a corporal drew the blinds in the carriages and we were ordered not to touch them. It was a military order and I obeyed.

The others were kept in Prague. Only I was handed over to a sergeant who had come to Prague on some errand, to get into another train and go farther east.

2

Sergeant Renner was middle-aged, clumsy, big. In the last war he had been wounded in the stomach and that made him unfit for drill. But he knew how to rule men. He had as many prejudices as there were hairs in his shabby moustache, and he was kind as well as arbitrary. All this I felt in the little he said during the journey. Afterwards I knew. When the train started, 'What's your name?' he said.

'Johann Reichel.'

'Hmm.' He gave me a sharp glance from small blood-shot eyes. 'When an officer asks you, answer, "Reichel, Johann." Have you had any food?'

'Four biscuits since yesterday.'

Lumbering from his corner, he fetched a canvas bag from the corridor, and among blankets and some ragged under-garments he found a parcel of cheese and bread. He divided it, giving me a half share. Then he went to sleep, his huge head falling forward, and sighed and grunted for the rest of the night.

At dawn the train stopped. We got out, Renner shaking himself like a bear, I numb with cold. There were fields, a stream, and, hanging over the village, hills covered in trees. There was a guard on the single platform, two men with machine-guns and four others pacing up and down. Renner spoke to them in his offhand way, and we left the station and plunged into air like fine glass, the sky clear and grey, and a narrow road beside the stream to the village. It was the same air as in Ruge.

I walked beside Renner, who said nothing. When he saw that I could swing myself along quickly and easily he quickened his stride and we walked the length of the village between fast-shut houses to a big house at the far end, nearest the hills.

Renner took me into a room where there were men on guard before a second door. There was a clock in the room and I saw that it was six o'clock. The second door opened, an officer in the uniform of the S.S. came through the room, and at once Renner, like the others, became rigid. I copied them. A voice from the inner room said, 'Sergeant Renner? Come in.'

3

When Renner beckoned me, I stood in the doorway and saluted. I had to walk the length of the room to the desk at the far end. The Colonel watched me come. Too tired to feel any fear, I looked at him: he was broad-shouldered, his face broad, with pale lips flattened against it, and grey eyes boring into my skull and emptying it of its few thoughts. There was neither kindness nor severity in the face. It was a landscape rather than a face, and I do not pretend to know what lived there.

'So they're sending me cripples now,' he said without seeming interested. 'Name?'

'Reichel, Karl Johann.'

'What can you do?'

What ought I to have said? I opened my mouth to say that I could do anything any other soldier could do, and said, 'I can ride and look after horses.'

'Excellent,' he said in the same voice. 'Can you write a legible hand? Can you add?'

'Yes, sir.'

He took a couple of papers from the pile on his desk.

'Copy this. Check the figures from the second sheet.'

Renner stepped forward and pointed me to a table against the wall. I sat down and began, my hands wooden with cold, to copy a long list of items, '20 pigs, 8 kegs butter…' I had no idea what it meant, and only later knew that I was listing the month's supplies sent from this district to Berlin, where they were badly needed in our war with England. I copied for two hours, then Renner took the papers from me, checked them, and sent me to find my own way to the mess.

When I was swallowing hot soup he came in and told me that I was to act as the Colonel's personal clerk. He said, 'You realise that it's a position of trust…What did you say your name was?'

'Johann Reichel.' I corrected myself: 'Reichel, Johann.'

Without a smile he said, 'If there's anything you

want to know, ask me, not one of the others. You are off duty now for five hours. You'd better sleep.'

I was too restless from excitement and too tired. I got up after half an hour of lying on my blanket and went outside to see what sort of place I was stationed in. By now a wintry sun shone.

It was a large farm, built round a courtyard. Standing in the yard, I could hear the stream, and stare up at the thickly wooded hills – dark green of firs and the thin young green of oaks, scarcely a veil yet, it was too early in the year. You could not say that it was like Ruge, but – one northern farm is never unlike another – the same smell of wet earth, herbs, stables. A sentry outside the stables let me look in at three fine horses, only fit for riding. They must, I knew, belong to the Colonel and the S.S. Lieutenant I had seen.

'Where does the Colonel ride?' I asked. I had a crazy vision of myself being called on to attend him as groom.

'He doesn't any longer,' the man said. He added drily, 'Ask no questions and you'll hear no lies.'

I went away and leaned against the gate leading from the yard into a rough orchard. At one side of the orchard were barns, and after a minute I saw that the nearer barn was lived in. A woman came to the door and poured out a little water on the ground. I heard a girl's voice. And suddenly I was sleepy, my eyes not able to keep open. I stumbled to the house and slept until a corporal woke me for duty.

On the second evening I had a chance to speak to Renner. He was mending a shirt. Not, as I knew already, that he cared how shabby he was, but he liked using his hands.

'Who lives in the barn?' I said.

He gave me one of his sharp glances: his face was so big and worn that to discover in it an arched delicate nose, the nose of an aristocrat, was a shock.

'Palivec,' he said calmly.

'Who?'

He interrupted me. 'Palivec was the mayor of the village. He's a farmer. He used to live in this house. To keep him more or less under his eye, Colonel Werder put him and his family in the barn when we took the house.' He paused, biting an end of the thread with discoloured teeth. 'For a Czech, he's not a bad chap at all.'

I had been two, nearly three days in the Protectorate, and I had not yet seen a Czech, except for the glimpse of a woman in the door of the barn. The evening before, when I wanted to go out and look at the village, I had been told it was forbidden to go alone.

'They're pretty fair brutes, aren't they?' I said.

Something in Renner's offhand voice made me feel small. He looked over my head.

'There's not much difference in human beings.'

To cover up my feeling of humiliation, I said, 'How many of them pig it in that barn?'

'I shouldn't think they pigged it,' he said drily. 'They seem very decent. There's Palivec himself, his wife, his son, his son's wife, his married daughter and her husband. And another daughter – a good deal younger than the others.' He looked at me again. 'If you're thinking of calling on them –'

His little joke made him laugh in a chuckling way that shook his loose heavy body.

4

I learned that our task was to guard the railway. It was the main east-to-west line, carrying men and supplies to the defensive zone in the east. There had been so many accidents at this place – the hills were ideally useful to Czech brigands – that two years ago Colonel Werder had been sent to stop them. When he came, half his men were S.S., young picked fighters, and the rest veterans of the other war, like Sergeant Renner. The Colonel himself began as an officer in the Imperial army. In the last few months every soldier under forty – that included all the S.S. – had been taken from him. Their places were filled by older men and 'defective parts'. One S.S. only was left – the Lieutenant.

This officer reminded me at sight of a schoolmaster in the Ruge school, a young man we children hated for his sarcasm. He never spoke to us except sneeringly, and when he punished he treated the culprit – I was going to write victim – to ten minutes biting irony first. Lieutenant Vogt spoke little, and was arrogant rather than sarcastic, but he had much the same type of face – smooth, with fine narrow features, colourless lips, light hair. It was he and not the Colonel who gave the villagers their first lesson in correct behaviour. The Colonel had gone home on leave, and the first night he was away, a patrol brought into the farm two Czechs they had picked up near the railway, long past the hour when the villagers were forbidden to leave their houses. The men said they were from another village, but they would not give their names. And in short, the

Lieutenant did not believe them. He and four of the S.S. questioned them all night in the ante-room to the Colonel's room. In the morning the Czechs were dead, or rather, one dead and the other dying, and the Lieutenant exposed them on a sort of cross, back to back, in the street outside the farm.

The soldier who told me about it did not like severities of this sort. That is, he approved of severity, but he thought it ought to take the form of shooting or hanging. Thinking about it, I was inclined to agree with him. But I am not sure how much the memory of our detestable schoolmaster affected me. There were other similar stories about Lieutenant Vogt. He had seized any chance, when the Colonel was absent, to impress his own idea of discipline on the village. Now that the S.S., except himself, had gone, he was less ambitious and worse-tempered, and his orderly had a bad time with him. I noticed — one day when he ordered me to come with him to the station — that any villager we met in the street turned into the nearest house to avoid passing him. This demonstration, if you can call it that, was meant certainly for Vogt. We others were only ignored.

I had no temptation to break any of the rules against fraternising with Czechs. The atmosphere in the village was stifling with dislike. That scarcely describes it. It was as though each of us Germans walked about in a cloud formed of his own breath. If I spoke to a villager — during a requisition of straw or food, perhaps — he answered, if it were a man, without glancing at me. The women looked you in the face, but with a sort of surprise and distaste which was not pleasant. I knew why Vogt struck one of them suddenly across the mouth when she was handing over her pillows. Yet I wished he hadn't.

One morning when I went into the courtyard I saw that the cherry trees in the orchard were coming into blossom. They were in that brief delicious stage when you see more buds than flowers and, when you look at the branches, more blue sky than whiteness. The air was full of a light scent of water and young leaves. I knew it so well. It was spring.

As I leaned on the gate, Palivec came out of his barn and came towards me. His women took a long way round to the village, but he was used to coming through the farm. I watched him coming for a moment, trying to think whom he reminded me of. He was a tall man, his head narrow, yet because of the big forehead and high cheekbones, it looked strong. When he was almost at the gate I stepped back and swung it open. I did it involuntarily. He halted, he must have supposed I was coming through into the orchard. Still holding the gate open, I said, 'Good morning.'

Palivec did not reply. After another moment he came on, passing me in the gateway.

'The sun is bringing on your trees,' I said.

He looked away from me as he answered, 'Last year I was able to supply you with five hundred kilos.'

He was walking through the gate as he said it, and he neither slowed nor quickened his long stride.

'Wait,' I said. He stood still.

I was confused. I knew that if anyone heard me I should have trouble in explaining what I was about. In fact I could not have given myself an explanation –

unless it was the likeness to someone I knew at home which was worrying me. Who was it? To cover up my insanity I said the first thing that came into my head.

'It's almost spring.'

Palivec did not turn his head towards me. In a calm voice he said, 'May I get on with my work?'

As he walked off, I shut the gate and went on staring at the cherry trees to give my face time to cool. I was raging with shame, anger, and extreme bewilderment. Why in the first place had I spoken to a lout of a Czech? And why, having been such a fool, was I vexed because I had failed to make him look at me when he answered?

Luckily, no one had seen the episode.

5

My work for the Colonel was exacting but not difficult. A never-dry stream of forms flowed out from Berlin to every local headquarters in the Protectorate – and I suppose into all the conquered countries. There must have been a vast Ministry in the capital working day and night to feed these thousands of streams. At our end sometimes it seemed a useless, at least an inessential, task. We made lists on demand of every conceivable thing, down to the chairs and cups in the village houses; lists of the things we had sent home; the things we expected to be able to send; reports on the crops; reports on every incident, trivial or not; finally, lists of the lists themselves. I was writing and copying ten and twelve hours a day. We had a typewriter but no one who could use it. Besides, it had broken down, and though at intervals the Colonel indented for another, and another was even promised, it never came.

The Colonel treated me, always, exactly as on the first day. He did not speak to or look at me as if I were a person; simply I was his writing hand. His glance when he gave an order passed over my face like an acid which obliterated my features. I thought he was not dissatisfied with me, but nothing he said – he said nothing, simply gave orders – gave me the right to think it. As for me, I admired him more than I could have admired anyone in the world, except the Leader. Naturally I guarded myself from letting a sign of my worship – it was that – show in my face or voice. It would have been an offence – even if it had been thinkable. His calm energy was remarkable. If, as happened sometimes, he worked through the night, neither his face nor his manner were fatigued. He carried, I think, the map of the country in his head. Now and then he had to advise Headquarters in Prague on some military operation. Then, to see his mind at work, a tiger able to think, was a fearful joy. I used to wonder why he was not in a more glorious place, and not a general. Catching Sergeant Renner alone one day, I asked him.

'There's such a thing as being too intelligent,' he said in his casual way. 'I'm not referring to you, Reichel. You're merely a case of arrested discipline. If I knew why our Colonel has remained a colonel I shouldn't tell you. As a matter of fact, I don't know. I did hear that he was too clever with some field marshal on one occasion, but I know nothing about it. Take my advice, and ask fewer questions.

Disregarding this – I was no longer afraid of Renner, though I had respected him all the more since one of the soldiers talked to me about his war record – I said, 'How did he succeed in stopping the accidents on this railway?'

For a moment Renner did not speak. He was sitting, knees apart, his big hands clasped between them loosely. His face wore that look of patience strangely mixed with pride which had struck me before. I think he was a well-educated man, though I never saw him reading. He was silent so long that I grew nervous. Our good Renner had an arbitrary temper. At last – I had been on the point of asking his pardon – he growled:

'There's no reason why you shouldn't know. I see no reason. What he did was quite simple. He called a meeting of the villagers and told them that if there was an accident he wouldn't waste time looking for brigands, he would simply shoot, at once, every man of twenty to twenty-nine years of age in the village. And if there was a second accident he would shoot the thirties to thirty-nines, and so forth. The Mayor – I mean Palivec – told him, very courageously, I thought, that none of the accidents had been the work of men living in the village, and that it was a brutal plan. Colonel Werder's answer was that he knew the brigands didn't live in the village, but they got help and information from villagers. Palivec tried to argue, and the Colonel said: 'Hold your tongue – if I have to shoot, you're responsible...' Yes. Yes, the accident was three months later. They derailed a troop train – very competently – killing two men. Oh, and holding up other trains, of course. The Colonel did what he'd said, the men were rounded up – I daresay some got away into the hills – there were thirty-one here in the yard. The Colonel came and looked them over, and said "I'm not going to waste the men's time swilling the yard. Take them to the other side of the orchard and shoot them there, do the ground good…"And so they were shot, with a machine-gun, in Palivec's orchard. Palivec was allowed to go with them; at the last minute he said something in his own language. One of the young men began to answer…'

Renner unclasped his hands, and began to rub the palm of one round his scalp – it was one of his gestures. 'It was effective. There hasn't been an accident in this district since.'

He had told the story drily and calmly, but I was trembling with excitement. I could see the Colonel as he looked at the Czechs – those eyes of his destroying face after face until a line of faceless anonymous bodies stood there.

'My God, he's a great man,' I cried.

Renner cocked one eye at me. 'Who?'

'The Colonel, of course. It was a magnificent thing to do.'

'How old are you?' Renner said.

'Twenty,' I said. 'Why?'

'Nothing, nothing,' he mumbled.

He yawned, and got up. Lurching like a bear, he went to his blanket and lay down. He used to lie on his back, awake, hands folded on his chest. He said he'd lost the habit of sleeping.

Next day when I was off duty for an hour in the afternoon, I went through the orchard and stood at the spot where I supposed the thirty-one had been killed. Were they buried here? I looked round. The grass was the same everywhere, and I thought how little difference it makes to the earth that men live a little and then die. No difference at all. Palivec's cherry trees don't know anything about the thirty-one young men stretched out under them. And then – no doubt the spring was disordering my mind slightly – I thought: But the young men may have had something to say, when they found themselves lying next to the roots of trees in the ground. That one who didn't finish his sentence, perhaps…The air was sweet this morning, and the trees masked by wave on wave of white flowers, whiter than foam. Foam is coarse beside the dazzling fineness of cherry-blossom.

I had nearly reached the gate into the courtyard when Palivec's younger daughter came out of their barn. I knew she was the unmarried one, she was a girl. I knew her name. Renner, who must – why? – have taken the trouble to find out a good deal about the Palivec family, dropped it in our talk. Marja. She was sturdy, very fair-skinned, with blue eyes and light hair-yellow. The devil, or the spring – I don't, of course, believe in the devil, except as we say 'English devil' – prompted me to speak to her.

'Your orchard is very fine.'

If she had said, 'No finer for you being in it,' or made any such insolent remark – or if she had curled her lip – I should have felt I had scored over her. She walked past me as though she had not heard me – as if I weren't even there. I felt myself crimson, and when I walked into the yard Sergeant Renner was waiting. He stopped me.

'You've been warned not to talk to villagers,' he said curtly.

'Yes, Sir,' I said. I had no excuse.

'Well – don't do it again.'

There was no kindness in his manner. I went back to work with the uncomfortable certainty that I was in disgrace with him.

Later in the afternoon the Colonel sent me, with one of the older men, to fetch a parcel from the station. I was glad to be out in the sun, and I began to feel better. That is perhaps why – although I had been vaguely conscious of something changed in the village – it was not until we were coming back that I realized what it was. The Czechs we passed looked at us.

I was so astonished that I seized my companion's arm. 'Did you see that?' I said.

He shook my hand off – he was a surly old boy. 'What?'

'They look at us…'

'Well, why shouldn't they?' he grumbled.

I looked at him. Yes, he felt it, too. He was not going to talk about it to a recruit – and a 'defective part' at that. When the next Czech passed us, I was ready for him. I stared back. The look in his eyes was like all the others, a mixture of hate and – yes – curiosity. It was this last that startled me.

'I shan't be sorry to leave this place,' I blurted.

My companion laughed in the jeering way these old soldiers laughed at us recruits. 'When d'you expect to leave?' he said.

'After we win the war,' I said. I was irritated.

In a different voice — soft, almost kind — he said, 'We shan't win the war.'

'Old fool,' I said to myself. It jumped into my mind that he was making fun of me. I shrugged my shoulders and said nothing, and we walked in silence past the white houses and under the trees leaning above the lane to the farm. I looked through the branches at a sky of clear burning blue. My heart leaped with happiness...

Sergeant Renner and I slept in a little room together above the Colonel's, so that he could rouse us at any hour by banging his stick on the ceiling. In the middle of that night we were wakened by one of the men on duty. There had been an accident to the night train.

6

I sat at my table in the Colonel's room, copying from Renner's scrawled list the names of the villagers who had been arrested during the night. They were shut in the big cellar, twenty-nine of them — the men from 'thirty to thirty-five'. The Colonel's first order had been 'thirty to thirty-nine'. Then, for some reason, he changed it.

He and Lieutenant Vogt were discussing it at his desk. They had the habit of talking freely in my presence — I might as well call it my absence, since the Lieutenant no more than Colonel Werder regarded me as a living or thinking object.

'Why not take the rest?' Vogt said.

The Colonel spoke in a drawling voice, as if Vogt bored him. I think certainly he didn't like him and his S.S. jerkiness.

'Because – now it's started again – it will go on, and we shall need hostages. Suppose we shoot too many men, the few left will feel indifferent.'

'With respect, sir, I don't see it.'

Colonel Werder looked once at the place where Vogt's face should have been.

'Suppose you were the wife of a man of thirty-six, you would prefer him, wouldn't you, to live? Well, tonight there will be more anxious wives in the village than if I removed every man up to thirty-nine. They'll know that thirty-six to forty come next on the list.'

The word list may have reminded him of me. He turned his head slightly: without looking up, I knew that his glance had rested for a second, not more, on my hands. I went on writing. I had just copied the name Jírko. Jírko, Vincenc. I moved my finger down Renner's list – it was easy to lose one's place among Czech names. Something turned quickly in my stomach. Next on the list came: Palivec, Jan. Palivec's son.

Lieutenant Vogt was saying, 'We could still shoot the wives.'

'If it should be necessary,' the Colonel said in the voice he used to close a conversation. Vogt went out.

At this moment I realised that I detested the S.S. Lieutenant as fervently as I admired Colonel Werder. Was it the contrast between the Colonel's god-like calm and Vogt's quick violent voice? No – Vogt was hateful in himself: he was smooth and impudent, he bullied his servant mercilessly, he treated Sergeant Renner with a rudeness which Renner withstood by an extraordinary air of detachment; he gave the Lieutenant no reason to complain of him, and yet there was a wall of indifference on Renner's side shutting him off from any possibility of being insulted by the S.S. officer. Strange, and true.

I glanced without moving my eyelids at the Colonel. His eyes were fixed, staring – as though whatever he was thinking about were a long way in the past or the future. Could he, I wondered, dissolve past and future events simply by looking at them? My heart ached with love – yes, love. If he had said to me, 'Reichel, take my revolver and blow your brains out,' I should only have felt happy.

One of the guards came in.

'Sir, the Czech Palivec is outside. He is asking permission to speak to you.'

The Colonel's face never showed a feeling – yet I imagined that he had expected Palivec.

'Send him in.'

Seeing them together, I saw that they were of an age. They were perhaps in the middle fifties – like, I thought, Renner. I realised, in the same instant, another thing: whatever Colonel Werder thought about Palivec – whether, I mean, he despised him as a savage or mistrusted him as a Czech, crafty as Czechs are – he did not dislike him. You cannot be anyone's slave, as I had made myself the Colonel's, without learning to read him by signs not perceptible to others. When the Colonel was at ease – it is not absurd to talk of him being at ease, I have seen him relaxed before a fine day, or watching the honey drip off his spoon on to bread – he tapped the little finger of his left hand on the arm of his chair. I am sure he had no idea that he did it. His face, as always, was heavily impassive. How they had trained themselves, or been trained, those officers of the old army, to show as little of their feelings as a stock! It was magnificent in its way. No other people I know of can have done it. Between the Colonel and Lieutenant Vogt was all the difference between discipline and fear. The Lieutenant was ashamed of any feelings he had, Colonel Werder had mastered his.

He told Palivec to sit down. Palivec hesitated. Not, I saw, because he was surprised, or diffident; but because he had no mind to sit with a German.

'I ask you to sit,' the Colonel repeated softly. His little finger tapped, lightly, briskly.

Palivec took a chair facing the Colonel across the desk.

'I know why you've come,' my Colonel said. 'You know that I'm going to shoot your men who are in the cellar under this room, you know it's a waste of time to argue about it. You've come to do something even more childish. You're going to ask me to let them off and shoot you.'

Palivec's eyebrows twitched. 'No,' he said, in a dry voice.

'I'm wrong?' The Colonel was staring in his face. He was surprised, I daresay, that it had not become a blank piece of flesh.

'Yes, you're wrong,' Palivec said. 'I'm a Czech, not a sentimental Prussian. I know the value of a soldier. An experienced soldier.'

He spoke good German, with the same abrupt precision as Sergeant Renner when he was talking in his natural, not his military, voice — Renner made less difference between them than you would expect.

'A year ago, six months ago, you wouldn't, if you were speaking to me, have called yourself a soldier — experienced or otherwise.' The Colonel's voice was as dry as Palivec's.

Palivec looked at him. 'Six months ago, though I knew Germany had lost the war — and you knew it — you would have laughed at me if I had said so. You won't give yourself the trouble of laughing today. I know, and you know I know, that your troops are being withdrawn from my country, back into Germany. Not only from this country they're going back but from every country in Europe. Here — so far — they haven't been molested. I don't know anything about other occupied countries.'

'You must want me to laugh,' the Colonel said calmly. 'How does even an experienced Czech — what is it you call them? — legionary? — guerrilla? — molest a German division?'

Palivec was looking down at his hands.

'Not all your outposts equal a division,' he said slowly. 'This is an outpost.'

I was listening, and pretending to write. My wrists felt weak. I had not taken in the sense of what Palivec said when he was speaking, and what stupefied me now was that the Colonel accepted his statement. My mind — my body, too — was numb. Shaking, and trying not to shake, I listened.

'Well,' my Colonel said.

Palivec leaned forward. 'I give you my word,' he

said, as coldly as if he expected his word to be taken, 'no soul in the village was involved in last night's accident. No one here expected it.'

'What has that to do with it?'

'What good will it do you,' Palivec said, 'to murder a few innocent Czechs — adding them to the others, innocent or not so innocent, you've killed since 1938? When you know as well as I do, better, I daresay, than I do, that you're at the end of your time here.'

Colonel Werder interrupted.

'Near the end, not at the end.'

'As you like,' Palivec said indifferently.

'You don't convince me. And I'm sure you didn't expect me to be alarmed.'

After a minute the Colonel added, 'You haven't mentioned that among the men in the cellar under us is your son.'

'My son-in-law, Vincenc Jírko, as well,' Palivec said quietly. 'I don't come to ask for their lives, more than for the lives of the others.'

'Why did you come?'

'Not even to bargain with you,' Palivec said. 'The safety of your — your outpost for our men's lives. I thought it just possible you would listen to reason — when reason is mercy.'

There was a silence. To my profound amazement, I noticed the Colonel's little finger, tapping, tapping. He lifted his head to look at Palivec — and shook it.

'No, my friend,' he said. 'You do your duty and I'll do mine.' He smiled — yes, smiled. 'You know that I've no other reason for living, except to do what I was trained to do.'

He pushed his chair back. Palivec got up. He stood for a moment, as if reflecting – and again I was plagued by his likeness to someone I must have seen somewhere. It eluded me again. He turned, and went out without looking at my Colonel: who watched him without a change in his face.

An hour or so later I was in the courtyard when four of the Czechs were fetched out of the cellar. Renner, who was there, handed out spades as though they were walking-sticks. With a guard of eight of our men, carrying rifles, they were marched not into the orchard, but into a field at the far side, away from the barn. It came over me that they were going to dig the graves for all of them, and I realised, in the same moment, with horror, that I did not want to see the shooting. The mere thought turned me up.

I may have shown it. Renner came over to me: he had a handful of papers, those eternal lists.

'I want a fair copy of these before twelve,' he said roughly. 'Get on with them.'

Shut in the Colonel's room, I heard the rest of the Czechs singing in their cellar, then Renner's voice, then their footsteps on the cellar steps, then silence. Then, after about ten minutes, the clatter of a machine-gun. I felt a sickening wrench in my body, as you do an instant before you fall. That's over, I thought – a stupid thought.

7

In the evening I ventured into the courtyard. There was a light cold wind, such as often came at that hour, after the warmth of the April sun. In the last day or two, the cherry-trees had lost their brightness and turned ragged, but against the wall of the barn there was a plum-tree coming into flower. I stood in the yard looking at it. You can understand that I felt disinclined to go into the orchard.

The door of the barn opened and the three Czech women came out. There was the mother, Palivec's small, grey-haired wife, and the two wives. Without lifting their eyes to the farm, they went towards the field. I had no wish to see them, but I stood there. Then other women began coming. They came along the way the Palivec women took when they wanted to go to the village – one alone, then two together, then one. None wept. They went past with perfectly dry eyes.

Suddenly one of them – the only one who did it – turned and looked at me as she passed the gate. I felt cold. Cold came to me from the Czech woman.

There is nothing else I can say.

8

A fortnight or so later – I was sitting at my table waiting for orders – Lieutenant Vogt came into the room, and the Colonel told him that armed bodies of Czechs had murdered all the men of two of our posts in a part of the country nearer the frontier.

'Where are they getting arms?' said Vogt.

The Colonel lifted his eyebrows. 'What do you think? Did you really suppose that either we or the police had unearthed every rifle and machine-gun hidden in cellars and caves?'

He spoke to me without turning his head. 'Get out. I don't want you just now.'

I went out and looked for Renner. He was in our room, at his favourite trick of mending some garment or other. Dear knows they needed it, his garments — and dear knows they looked no better for his efforts.

'Is this an outpost?' I asked him. 'How is it an outpost?'

'I shouldn't call it an outpost,' he said. 'I should call it a cover-post. So long as troops and supplies are being brought back along the railway, we stay here and try to prevent accidents. See?'

I went over to the window. It was a small window, we had propped it open; from it you saw the valley, the stream, the church no larger than a barn, the houses marching from it one way to the hills and another to the stream and the road leading to Prague. It was half in the sun and half in the shadow of a white cloud.

'And when shall we be brought back?' I had my back to Renner. He was a time answering, and I turned round. He looked at me — his big unkempt head tilted back, eyes half-shut with — indifference and kindness.

'Never,' he said softly. 'We shall never get home.'

I revolted against his words. No — that is too violent — I knew that I, at any rate, was not going to die. I felt too strong and alive. Yet for all I knew — I say, knew — that my life could not end, he had given me a deep shock.

'Why do you say such things?' I cried.

'I thought you asked me,' he said in his casual way.

I was hurt and angry. It seemed to me shameful, if we were in such danger, that he sat there fiddling with a patch on one of his two shirts. He was attending more to his patch than me.

'Isn't there anything we can do?' I said.

'What do you mean?' he said with a slight smile. 'My poor Reichel, a great many men as young as you have been certain they wouldn't be killed. The only thing to do is not to tell oneself any lies.' He gave me a friendly sly look. 'I shan't say this to any of the others.'

He couldn't have found words better designed to steady me. I began to feel another sort of confidence – not so much in myself as in the company. With officers like the Colonel and Sergeant Renner, what could go wrong with us? I remembered that it was more than a fortnight since I had written home, and I got out my notebook and began – 'My dear little mother…'. There I stuck, my brain when I tried to go on felt positively leathery. The more I dragged at it, the more I ran against things it was impossible to tell her. Could I tell her I might never see her and Ruge again, or about the shooting? I struggled with a sentence or two, and gave up.

Renner had watched me absently. When I put the paper away, he said, 'In your reports – I mean, in the Colonel's reports – have you come across a fellow called Milos the Soldier? A Czech, of course.'

'No.'

Renner looked away. 'He must have written his own report about it,' he muttered.

'Well, who is this Milos?' I asked.

'I don't know,' Renner said. 'It seems there's a fellow calling himself Milos the Soldier – not just Milos – a sort of leader, inside the country. Not one of those fellows who have been fighting and cursing outside. He's been very busy and very clever. So clever that though it's known he exists, and is probably at the bottom of a good deal of the mischief these Czech devils make, no one has run him to earth.' He yawned. 'I thought you might have seen something. I must say I admire a chap who risks his life that way.'

9

I avoided going through the village. There is something worse than being ignored, that is being loathed. Not merely hated – loathed – as though one is something too vile to be touched. When I could not get out of my turn of duty at the station, I walked past the Czech houses feeling that any moment a door would open and a woman stand there and look at me as the woman looked the day of the shooting. The more I tried to stiffen myself – after all, what are Czechs? – the more sore and humiliated I felt. Also, I was afraid. It is shameful, but true. For the first time since I came, the thought that we were a company, only a handful, of German soldiers set down in the middle of a hostile country, weighed on me. Not simply the people and their village, but the trees, the river, the hills, were enemies.

I still went into the orchard. Dead Czechs can't do

any harm, I thought. But to show you the state of mind I was in now – the afternoon when I fell there, my instant panicky thought was of a hand stretching up through the grass to grasp my ankle. I got up quickly – and collapsed again, cursing. I had wrenched my sound ankle, and now, with both of them gone, I was lamer than any cripple. I looked at it. It had swelled, and the pain when I tried to walk made me set my teeth. Helping myself from tree to tree, I walked back. When I had to pass the barn there were no more trees, and I moved as painfully as a crushed snail, praying to God that no one came out.

It was the girl who came out. Marja. From the corner of my eye I saw that she started forward, then drew back. Yes, yes, I thought, it's a lame man but it's a German. I dragged on. Suddenly I felt giddy, and stumbled. I stopped. She had watched all this, that Marja, without moving.

I was startled when she spoke. Such a clear voice!

'Have you always been lame?'

'Not like this,' I muttered.

'But you *are* lame?'

'My right foot.'

'Are there many lame German soldiers?'

This mockery was spoken in a cool, almost friendly voice. I did not answer. I should have gone on – I felt better – but I longed for her voice, her girl's voice, to say a few more words in precise simple German – like a well brought-up German child. I felt the sun on the back of my head, and there was a light scent of lilacs. I could not see the tree and turned my head to look for it.

'Where are your lilacs?' I asked.

'Behind the barn.'

She turned away as soon as she had said it, back into the barn, and the door shut. The sun, which had been a German sun for a second, turned Czech again, like the cherry trees, the lilacs I couldn't see, the air, the dry ground under my feet. I got back to the house, and had my ankle bandaged. One of the men found a stick for me to hobble about with, and so I got on. At night I was glad to lie down.

I don't know how long I had been asleep when it started. There were first shouts I heard in my sleep, then Sergeant Renner's foot in my side rousing me, then the shots… Renner grumbled, 'The light's gone. Damn it, why haven't I my torch?' There were only two torches in the company; one of them had been Renner's; the Lieutenant took it from him when his own failed and no more batteries or torches came with the supplies… I was feeling in the dark for my tunic, the only garment I took off at night now. I found it, and my stick and rifle, and stumbled out on the stairs.

The darkness was full of confused noise and shots. I could hear a man screaming outside, and suddenly the lights came on, on the landing and in the ante-room. I was on the lowest stair now, I dropped my stick and began to fire off my rifle at two men. I don't think I hit either before I felt the blow from a fist on the side of my head. It echoed in my head in a blackness.

I found I was on the floor of the Colonel's room. I sat up. No one took notice of me. I could look round. There were about a dozen of our men, nine of the old soldiers and the rest 'defective parts', legs and hands bound; Lieutenant Vogt, roped to a chair; the Colonel, leaning against the desk, his hand gripping his left arm; a trickle of blood came through his fingers. And there, close to me, lying on the floor with his knees in his stomach, just as he always slept, my poor Renner. In spite of the war and the shootings, he was the first dead man I had seen in my life. He was not horrible, he was only pitiful and majestic with his big forehead and arched nose; his mouth was clenched. Beside him lay a dead Czech, with a hurt angry face, young, almost a child.

Czechs, Czechs with rifles – one with a machine-gun – were between us and the door. The ante-room was filled with them. By now I knew many of the villagers by sight. These men were not from the village except for one big gaunt man we called the Englishman, because he had lived in America and spoke their dog's language.

Palivec came in.

He looked at our dozen soldiers and said, 'Take them into the stable and hang them with the others. Don't waste ammunition on them.'

One of the Czechs pulled me to my feet. Palivec noticed me then for the first time. 'Have you your first aid?' he asked me.

When I tried to answer my tongue was too thick and heavy for me to move it, but I took out the little roll of lint and the stuff like cotton waste they said was really wood or glass, I forget which.

'Bandage your officer,' he said.

One of our 'defective parts' was crying bitterly

when they went out. I ripped the Colonel's sleeve with his own pocket-knife, and did what I could with a gash from which blood and fleshy yellow cells had oozed. I was worried, trying to recall what I had been taught during my week in Berlin about first aid, and I forgot – almost – that this was the Colonel's arm I was touching. When I remembered, a feeling of pure joy shot through me.

'Are you in pain?' Palivec asked him.

'No,' my Colonel said. 'A little.' He was as controlled as usual. 'How many people have you here?'

'Fifteen hundred.'

'You thought it would take that many, did you?'

Palivec almost smiled. Then he turned to Vogt, sitting bound to his chair. His face turned a grey stone colour, his eyes moved a very little in their pits – I thought of a snake I had seen at Ruge, ready to kill. Even his voice had altered.

'You,' he said. 'You wretched murderer. Do you remember making a cross of Karel and Petr? Do you remember?'

There were a number of other things he invited the S.S. lieutenant to remember. Some of them I would rather not remember myself. But Vogt gave no sign of hearing what Palivec said. I daresay Palivec noticed this. He paused and said, 'It wouldn't be any use our torturing you, nothing we could bring ourselves to do would be enough. You will be beheaded.'

And that is what they did. They untied the Lieutenant and made him kneel across a stool in the doorway to the ante-room, and two of the Czechs held him while the 'Englishman' tried to detach the bayonet from his rifle.

It did not come off, and another Czech handed over his. Oh God, I prayed, let me die now. I looked at the Colonel. He was calm. He kept his eyes steadily on the doorway. They were wide open and seemed paler than ever. He had spoken to Vogt when they were loosening him from his chair, and Vogt only said, 'Yes.' He said nothing else, until when the knife was working on his neck, he screamed, and went on for an endless minute. The Colonel's eyes did not move – as if he had sworn it to himself or to Vogt.

My sight went. I fell and fell, into blackness and confused noise.

I came back into a light that seemed very vacant and cold. After a moment I realised that it was the early morning coming into the room through a window that was swinging open. I turned my head. There were two, only two people in the room, the Colonel and Palivec. They had taken away Sergeant Renner and the Czech boy. The door into the ante-room was closed. Palivec and my Colonel were sitting down, facing each other, as on that other day, across the desk. How long, I wondered dully, had they been facing each other? From the quiet way they talked it might have been a long time, hundreds of years. The Colonel was speaking.

'...nor have you solved anything, my friend. And what you are beginning again no one knows. You least of all.'

'We have not had our orders for the future,' Palivec said. He lifted one of his long hands. 'Not yet. Where does the end of terror and torment lead – the end of German protection? I don't know of any precise road

– but to something you have no idea of, you a German. Acceptance of freedom, love for the common, the humble, the weak. Why do you smile?'

'I don't understand you.'

'How could you?' Palivec said softly. 'Our grandchildren may understand each other – you've seen to it that I have no sons to understand yours, if you have a son. The blood between you and all other peoples in Europe is too wide a flood for you to hear what I'm saying.'

My Colonel's shoulders jerked. He looked across the room and said in his driest voice, 'I'm dying of sleep. That's not your intention, is it?'

Palivec pushed his chair back. He stood up.

'Do you know who I am?'

'I began to suspect it yesterday.'

'Only yesterday?' I thought Palivec sounded a little vexed.

'If I'd suspected sooner, you wouldn't be talking to me today. I was going to arrest you today and get rid of you, to make sure.'

'It wouldn't have made any difference,' Palivec said slowly. He began to walk towards the door. 'You understand,' he said over his shoulder, 'I couldn't spare you even if I wanted to – and I don't know that I do. But you put too many of us to bed in my orchard.'

'I did what I had to,' the Colonel said drily. 'There's only one way to keep order.'

Palivec stood still.

'Why were you keeping it in my country? You weren't invited.'

'Don't let's begin again,' the Colonel said, smiling.

43

'Why? Don't you want to know what I'm going to do to you?'

'Do it.'

Palivec had his hand on the door. He pulled it open, and at once four Czechs who must have been waiting there like proper sentries came in. Palivec jerked his head.

'Take Colonel Werder into the orchard. Shoot him.'

The Colonel stood up. It came over me that it was my turn next. I struggled to sit up, but I was dizzy and fell back against the wall. I felt nothing except the most terrible longing for him to speak to me. One word – one single encouraging word. Then I shouldn't be afraid.

'My Colonel,' I cried.

He was stepping past me; his eyes passed over my face – wiping it out. He was completely indifferent. I might not have been there.

I watched him go out. Now I was alone. I shut my eyes. The darkness that filled my mind was nothing so pleasant and kind as unconsciousness: it was the darkness all over Europe, the dark of the night when Germans are killed. We had gone into every country, we had covered Europe like a flood; now, when we were going back, the outposts everywhere, men like us, left without reinforcement, stranded without help miles from Germany, were lost. The people would rise in all the countries, to kill us Germans as we went back or stood. Dark, it was dark everywhere.

I held my eyes open, and saw Palivec standing by the desk. Perhaps I imagined the trace of regret on his face; if it were there it was the merest trace. A crazy thing to think at the time, but it came into my head that he and the Colonel had had one joke they both understood that no one else did, and now he would have to keep it to himself all his life. I heard rifle shots. Palivec lifted his head. The light was strengthening and warming. It must have been nearly sunrise.

Then – I had not heard her coming – Palivec's wife came in the doorway. She stood there, with that look of patience and deep tiredness in her face.

'Can we begin cleaning the house now?' she asked her husband.

'Yes,' Palivec said absently.

He turned his head, and seemed for the first time to recognise me. He came and bent over me – and now I knew who it was he was like. If my father had lived into his fifties he would have had the same face, narrow, the eyes sunk behind big cheekbones, the long mouth. It was not a close likeness but it was very clear.

'Can you walk?' he said.

I tried again without success to get up. Palivec stooped and picked me up easily. I can't say that I hoped anything in this moment, but certainly I resigned myself.

He carried me across the yard to the barn, and dropped me on a bed – his own, I think. 'Anna,' he called. His daughter came in quickly – you could see that he was used to being obeyed. 'Look at this boy's leg.'

I cannot remember what I thought about while the Czech woman was bathing my wrenched ankle in water with a handful of herbs in it. I think I must just have felt at peace, not surprised nor, so far as I honestly remember, afraid or awkward.

I must have stayed there a week – longer. My ankle was bathed. I was fed – always in this room. Usually Anna brought me my soup and bread, but once it was Palivec's wife, who looked at me gravely and said something in Czech which did not sound harsh. There seemed always people coming and going in the courtyard, and once when I had the curiosity to look out I saw it full of Czechs with machine-guns – they seemed to be camping there. Marja I never saw. I heard her laugh once. It must have been her laugh.

I don't think I troubled much about my future. One evening Palivec came in. I stood up.

'Can you walk?' he said briskly. 'Good. You'll leave tomorrow.'

He went out before I could ask a question. I was still standing against the little window when the door opened again. There was Marja. She came a step or two into the room.

'Where am I to go?' I said.

'Wherever you came from,' she said in her light voice.

'Home?'

'I suppose so.'

My mind cleared suddenly. 'Why haven't I been shot or hanged?'

There must have been a sarcastic note in my voice, though God knows I had no right to use it with her. A hot colour came into her face.

'We're sending you home for you to remember that it would have been better if you had not been born – since you were born German,' she said softly. She turned to go.

'Don't go,' I exclaimed.

The door shut on her. I saw her again next morning, when I was leaving. When I looked at her, she turned her head aside.

I was wearing clothes Palivec had fetched me that morning. I think they were his son's. 'You'll be safer on the road in these than in a German uniform,' he said indifferently. 'You're not in much danger from Germans, mighty few of them are walking along the roads and they're not in a mood to shoot. When Czechs stop you, show them this paper.' He gave me a piece of paper with a few lines written in Czech. I hadn't the courage to ask what they meant. I tried to thank him.

'No, go,' he said, 'go.'

10

How long was I tramping on the road towards Prague? Weeks? Days? I didn't count and I don't remember. I showed my paper in villages. The man or woman who read it looked at me, some with distaste, some inquisitively, one or two even with kindness. They let me sleep in outhouses, and gave me food, and once a cup of wine. And then one morning when I was walking – it had rained and the air smelled of it and the wet grass – a lorry filled with Czechs drew up in front of me, and one of them beckoned. I handed up my paper. It passed from hand to hand, while heads poked over the edge of the lorry to look at me, and finally an officer of sorts sang out in sharp German, 'Get in. We'll take you to Prague.'

I climbed in, awkwardly because of my foot. Two of them helped me, but when I was in, and the lorry started, they took no more notice of me. Towards evening we came to Prague. There was a castle, I remember, and crowds in the streets, women walking with bundles in their arms as if they had so much to do they could not walk slowly. And at a corner three or four children in khaki jackets singing in their language. They waved at the lorry, and the soldiers shouted.

We stopped outside a barracks. The officer spoke to me. 'Wait. You don't belong here.'

'May I have my paper back?' I asked.

He gave it me, with a quick smile. After a few minutes, two soldiers came and hustled me along between them to a building in another street, and into a large room where there were hundreds of my countrymen, waiting like me to be sent home. One of them could translate my safe-conduct for me.

'The bearer is to be spared because he is a cripple, he is to be pitied because he is a German, signed, Milos the Soldier.'

I sat down in the large room, among the others. I was trying to think of Ruge, to see it as it must look now in spring. Shall I ever, I thought, be happy? Another thing came into my head. I shall never marry anyone, I thought.

A Love Song For Miss Lillian

Mark McWatt

When he received Daphne Shepherd's invitation to 'tea' on the afternoon of Friday next, Raymond Rose's first thought was that he would politely decline. Daphne Shepherd was herself quite pleasant company: a dear old friend of his late mother, she was bent on keeping up the social standards of polite Georgetown society in these much diminished times; but she also cultivated the friendship of a few government ministers as well as that of those eternally gloomy university academics who regularly berated the politicians and their policies in letters to the press. Raymond was not sure he wanted to be caught up in the arguments and recriminations of these two groups. It was true that Alister Shepherd, Daphne's husband, would pounce on the chance to 'rescue' Raymond by proposing a tour of his beloved orchid collection, but an hour's lecture on the fastidious needs and habits of the most recently blooming phalaenopsis was not Raymond's idea of an exciting way to spend a Friday afternoon...

When Daphne telephoned to find out whether he would be coming on Friday (Raymond having 'put off' the duty required of him by the R.S.V.P.), he hastened to explain, in a suitably apologetic tone, that he was in the middle of some very delicate and stressful negotiations having to do with the firm, and was not sure he could spare the time. Daphne tut-tutted and complained that he was in danger of becoming one of those dull young men whose only concern was their work, insisting that, if humanly possible, he should show up for her 'tea'. Raymond had to promise that he would do his best.

The 'delicate negotiations' were not just an excuse conjured out of nowhere, because Raymond was indeed involved in negotiating the purchase, for himself, of a senior partnership – in fact *the* senior partnership – in what used to be his father's old law firm, Rose, Robinson and Waaldijk. Working mostly on his own since his return from law school six years ago, he had quickly built up both a profitable practice and an enviable reputation, partly because he permitted himself few social or romantic distractions. The gossip was that he lived the life of a monk in the large family home he had inherited. At thirty-one he was still quite young, but everyone had expected great things of the son of Mr Jefferson Rose, who had died prematurely and tragically of leukaemia at the height of his career, only eighteen months after he had been appointed to the bench. Lawrence Waaldijk, the famous courtroom maverick and the bane of magistrates and judges (he had been censured on several occasions by the Bar Association), had been ailing and in semi-retirement for three years and the firm was being held together by the hard-working Norris Robinson, who was himself past the age of retirement. Apart from these, there were a number of junior partners, youngsters of

Raymond's generation. It had always been Robinson's idea that Raymond should be part of the firm, working his way up from the bottom, but Raymond, while agreeing from the beginning to be 'associated' with his father's firm, had decided that what he really wanted (once he'd acquired the money and the experience) was to take over the firm entirely – hence the 'negotiations'.

The deal was concluded on Thursday morning and Raymond was elated. That evening he decided he would go to Daphne's tea the following afternoon, feeling able to take on, in his euphoria, the glib politicians and the dyspeptic academics. So it was that at 5.30 on Friday evening he was seated in the large veranda of the Shepherd home in Bel Air Park, devouring one of Daphne's delicious shrimp patties and sipping her home-made soursop juice which, in his judgment, made the afternoon worthwhile.

'I know you can't resist my soursop punch, Raymond my dear,' Daphne said loudly. 'Your father was just the same, although your mother never could acquire the taste…' Then she leaned closer to him and whispered: 'I have a bottle of it in the fridge for you to take home, but don't let any of the others know.'

Raymond was really glad that he had come, for not only was the food and drink to his liking, but good old Daphne had thought of everything. True the politicians and academics were there (his entrance had interrupted a heated exchange between the minister of health and a professor of sociology well known for his research into prostitution in Georgetown), but he'd noticed at once the presence, in a corner of the veranda, of Mr Justice Ramcharitar, whom he had known from childhood as Uncle Ram, and whom he admired and respected. He had settled at once into the little wrought-iron chair next to him. As they sat sipping their drinks and munching on Daphne's snacks, Raymond began to tell Uncle Ram about his takeover of the law firm.

'Oh yes, I heard all about it from Norris,' the judge informed him. 'I think you should consider yourself damn lucky. Anyway, Norris is pleased; he thinks the firm is in good hands and he can retire in peace.'

'I think he believes I behaved shabbily at the outset.'

'Oh, you probably did, but you're the son of Jeff Rose and that means that Norris will forgive you anything – short of physical assault. Your father was his idol.'

Raymond was happy to hear this as he worried that he had perhaps been a little too tough and uncompromising in concluding the deal. Just at that point, however, Daphne swept onto the veranda accompanied by a woman of stunning beauty who immediately commanded everyone's attention, including Raymond's, despite the greying hair that signalled that she was at least in her mid-fifties.

'Now let's see, Lillian my dear,' Daphne said, 'whom haven't you met? Does everyone know Lillian de Cunha, my neighbour from down the street?' And the woman went around the small gathering, kissing cheeks or shaking hands with the other guests. She seemed to have brought with her a kind of excitement, a sense of drama that enlivened the atmosphere.

Raymond took it that this was because of her striking appearance and her poise. He stood and held out his hand as she approached him.

'Oh, Lillian, this is Raymond, Raymond Rose, the young lawyer who's been winning all his cases and setting the women's hearts afire – not that he pays them any mind…'

'Well, I know about him from reading the papers,' the woman said, taking his hand. 'It's so good to meet you,' and, as she looked into his eyes, Raymond thought he detected a flicker of anxiety – it was there for the briefest of moments and then gone, banished by her smile and what seemed to Raymond an almost professional charm. He was intrigued, not just by the woman and what he imagined he'd seen in her eyes, but also by his own reaction. He had never really been excited by a woman; he'd had several female friends and a few sexual partners over the years, but none of these relationships had become serious nor prolonged, precisely because his feelings always seem to have been engaged only on the surface. There were times when he'd begun to wonder if he was capable of commitment to a serious and lasting relationship – or even capable of falling in love – whatever that meant. The only thing he was certain about was that it had never happened to him.

As he had looked into the eyes of this woman, Raymond had the strange sensation that he was renewing an old and clandestine acquaintance. He felt both a twinge of excitement and the simultaneous conviction that this was quite absurd, since he had never met the woman. She moved on to greet others in the room and Raymond resumed his seat, but did not immediately resume his conversation with Judge Ramcharitar, as he was lost in thought, besieged by unfamiliar emotions.

'You seem quite taken with Miss Lillian, my boy,' the judge said. 'But then you're a man, no different from…'

'Miss Lillian,' Raymond repeated the phrase, as though tasting it in his mouth for the first time in ages. 'You know, I'm sure I've heard that name before, but I can't remember…'

'I'm sure you have, my boy, although you are really a generation too young to be fully aware of what it means. Miss Lillian is what would have been known in a previous age as a "courtesan". She was – some say still is – Georgetown's most famous courtesan. She is certainly its most beautiful. I suppose that she now belongs to an era, a world that is fast fading.'

'You mean she's a prostitute?'

'Come, come, my boy, one would never use that term to describe Miss Lillian; she's too beautiful, too refined: her traffic in the pleasures of the flesh is too delicately managed and too intricate and exciting for such a word to describe it justly. A prostitute is what our professor friend over yonder writes about: one of those desperate and brutalised women who pose along certain streets late at night hoping to be picked up by men cruising in their cars – women who are as likely to be repaid for their favours with a beating as with money. Miss Lillian would not be caught dead in such a scenario. No, "courtesan" is a much better word; she is, after all, a lady…'

Raymond was only half listening to this, for his eyes followed Miss Lillian around the veranda; he noticed the style with which she moved, greeted people, tossed her head and laughed, inclined her head conspiratorially towards the ear of a smiling politician, as if to impart a tastefully risqué reminder about a shared experience in the past. When she had disappeared inside to visit Daphne's tea-table, Raymond continued to see her in his mind, his frisson of excitement now heightened by what the judge had said. And he could not escape the haunting familiarity of the name, as it repeated itself in his head. He had definitely heard someone say 'Miss Lillian' long ago — perhaps one of his more worldly and knowing high-school classmates, passing on the prurient gossip of the time that fuelled their teenage fantasies.

'Well, boy, I can see you're still most impressed with our courtesan,' the judge said, rising from his chair. 'I'm afraid I have to run: Indra is having a few people over for dinner — that's why she isn't here — and I promised to be home in time to give her a hand. Must go and plead with Daphne to release me.'

As he saw the judge walk through the glass doors in quest of Daphne, Raymond was uncertain what he should do. If he remained in his chair in the corner he would feel isolated and awkward, but as he looked around he did not see a group he cared to join. In his mind swirled the exciting thought of Miss Lillian, but he felt panic at the possibility that she might emerge onto the veranda and choose to sit next to him. As it happened, he soon saw Alister Shepherd, ever the thoughtful host, coming over to keep him company.

Noting that it was already quite dark outside, Raymond thought it was safe to ask: 'Well, Alister, how are the orchids doing?'

'Oh, very well, thank you, Raymond. Ramcharitar always thinks that he's in his courtroom and must be the first to leave – it's a wonder he doesn't require us all to rise! Anyway, seeing you quite abandoned in the corner here, I thought I'd come over and keep you company for a while – or better yet,' he said, suddenly eager, 'come with me, I want to show you something.'

'Not your orchids,' Raymond said with a frown; 'it's too dark outside.'

'No, no – well in fact yes! But it's not what you think – oh, just come, for heaven's sake,' he said, and got up and moved towards the door. Raymond could only follow.

As they got to the sliding doors to the living room, they stood back to let Daphne and Miss Lillian pass onto the veranda, Raymond being again struck by the latter's poise and beauty. Alister Shepherd took Raymond into his study, took a book out of a desk drawer and handed it to him.

'Advanced copy; just got it yesterday. What do you think?'

It was a soft-bound book, very well produced, with a wonderful, glossy cover: *Orchids of Guyana*, by Alister Shepherd and Tony Cole; the front cover below the title was divided into nine squares, each a colour photograph of a flowering orchid.

'This is wonderful, Alister,' Raymond said, 'very handsomely produced. I had no idea that you were working on this.' He turned the book over to read the blurb on the back.

'I'd mentioned to Tony years ago that we should do it,' Alister said, beaming, 'but you know how these things are – neither of us did anything for years; then I met this photographer chap…'

Alister droned on as Raymond read the back cover and flipped through the colour photographs inside. It really was an impressive reference work and Raymond was disposed to revise his opinion of Alister as a pleasant but boring dilettante. He noticed that there were orchids in the book named after him – and after Tony. But when he handed the book back and Alister pulled out a box file and insisted on showing him all the photographs that did *not* make it into the book ('too costly, you know – all of this glossy colour photography'), and went on at great length about the history of its production, Raymond's positive feelings dwindled and he said that he really had to go.

He realised that he had been in Alister's study for over half an hour and when they returned to the veranda about half the guests had already left. Raymond went around saying his goodbyes. When he got to Miss Lillian, she smiled and extended her hand and Raymond found himself doing an extraordinary thing: instead of shaking hands, he took the hand and, bending over, pressed it to his lips.

'It's wonderful to meet you, Miss Lillian,' he heard himself say. As he kissed the hand, a faint whiff of some exquisite perfume reached his nostrils, seeming to convey the promise of sensual delights far beyond his limited experience. Her smile widened, but again Raymond thought he saw a flash of anxiety in her eyes – though nothing disturbed the surface of her charm and self-possession. Raymond thought he had begun to glimpse, for the first time, all that the word 'woman' could mean.

Daphne saw him to the stairs, handing him his bottle of soursop punch, wrapped in a plastic bag. 'Thanks for coming,' she said. 'It wasn't so bad, was it? You should get out more often, Raymond, you can't work all the time.'

When Raymond Rose got home that evening he felt restless. A ripple of disturbance had crept into his calm and carefully ordered life. He had always been self-analytical and keenly aware of his moods and the feelings and the circumstances that influenced them. He wondered how his carefully cultivated sense of security had come to be threatened. It was 'Miss Lillian', he knew, but in what sense? It was absurd to imagine that he was in love with her; she was twice his age; besides, it seemed to him to be something more *personal* than love, though he was not sure what that meant. He reasoned that it couldn't be his perception of her sexual attractiveness and availability. It was true that Judge Ramcharitar's discussion of her was mildly arousing, but Raymond had always prided himself on his resistance to the imperatives of the flesh. He enjoyed sex when it happened. He'd had various 'visiting relationships', but nothing for which he felt he could give up his 'freedom' – his desire to be in control of his life at all times. So it couldn't be that he had just been ambushed by sexual desire or succumbed to a 'feminine mystique' that he had never experienced before, or really believed in.

Some time after midnight he was in bed, but unable

to sleep. 'Miss Lillian', he heard someone say inside his head. Suddenly he sat upright in bed; he got up, turned on the light and held his head in his hands. It came back to him in waves, a childhood memory, something that he had not thought about in years. He walked down the dark corridor in his pyjamas to what used to be his parents' room, before he'd remodelled the house five years ago. He stood at the door, transported in memory to his childhood. He pushed the door ajar: the room was quite different now, a guest room with twin beds with identical green, patterned bedspreads; but he could see, in his mind, his parents' double bed against the far wall, with its mosquito net let down around it. His mother sat at her mirrored bureau across from the bed, her hair loosened, her pale blue nightgown almost transparent. His father sat on the edge of the bed in pyjama trousers, the net against his bare back. Now the room was half-lit by a street-lamp out on the road, but then there had been the warm yellow glow of a bedside lamp.

'It's no use, Jeff,' his mother was saying, 'I know all about her.'

His father sighed and said nothing.

'I'll say this for you,' his mother continued, 'you go for the best...nothing but the best. She's beautiful, and dressed in the best of everything...the best there is, but still a *whore*!' She spat out the last word with a venom that had startled the eight-year-old boy at the door, who did not understand all that she was saying, but read infallibly her feelings as she said it.

'It's late,' his father said; 'I'm in court tomorrow; can we discuss this another time?'

'Why, Jeff? Why do you throw me aside for that…that…Miss Lillian? Miss Lillian who makes all the husbands avert their eyes and wink and snicker at the mention of her name – and makes all the wives nervous, imagining, knowing that many of their husbands visit her…Oh Jeff, I thought we were beyond that…Why?'

'Yes, why?' his father had said, his voice rising. 'Ask yourself why. Why on earth would a man with a beautiful wife, a young son, a good home and a promising career go rooting, like a stray dog among the market bins, for scraps of sexual favour? Ask yourself why? – and look good into that mirror as you ask…' Raymond had watched his father get up from the edge of the bed and walk over to the open window. Looking out he had continued: 'One child, *one child!* And sex becomes boring, irrelevant, something to be gratefully transcended…It has served its purpose…That may be how *you* feel, but for me it's different…I'm still a young man, I still smoulder with the desire that you are no longer willing to satisfy… But it's late. I'm in court tomorrow…'

The child Raymond hears his mother's terrible sobs and watches her body shudder on the stool in front the bureau. He starts to scream outside the bedroom door, and feels the scalding urine run down his legs onto the floor. They both rush towards him…

The adult Raymond gently closed the bedroom door, as though closing the covers of a long-lost children's book he had just found and reread, only to be disturbed by a fairytale he had not thought about in years – and he would have laughed at the suggestion that its terrors could still affect him. He went back to his room and back to bed, 'Miss Lillian...Miss Lillian' in his head.

The next morning, after sleeping fitfully, Raymond lay in bed thinking. Another memory awoke. He is eleven; it is the day of his father's funeral. The graveside is full of lawyers and judges, everybody in black, men and women. Raymond himself is in a little black suit: his first suit is a funeral suit, and he only ever wore it once. It is very sad, everybody looks sad; his father died young of a terrible disease. His mother is trying to be strong. She holds onto his hand but he can feel the dry sobs that shake her body. He looks up at her face: it is hard, determined. She has become that terrible thing, a widow. Raymond and his mother are among the last at the graveside. There is a figure in black waiting in the distance, under a tree; she was not at the graveside during the burial, but as the last group is leaving she approaches slowly. His mother's grip tightens on his hand and she drags Raymond to one side so as to pass close to this other figure, walking in the opposite direction. As they pass, Raymond is not looking, but he hears his mother spit. They do not stop. He looks back and sees the other woman stop and take a handkerchief from her purse; she wipes her face without turning around. Raymond has not seen her face. When they get home he overhears Uncle Lawrence say to his mother in the kitchen: 'I know you're upset, dear – and she should never have gone there – but you should not have done it...to demean yourself like that!'

'The nerve of that Miss Lillian!' was all his mother said.

Miss Lillian lived in an extraordinary fever in Raymond's mind for the next few weeks. He went over and over his memories, as though he were preparing a difficult case for trial. He juxtaposed his recent memory of the elegant and stunningly beautiful woman he had met with the dim memory of his father and his mother's sad, hard face. He now discovered that somewhere deep inside he had always admired the woman in black at the graveside for not saying a word, not turning around, just taking out the hanky and wiping the face he could not see. There were times when he felt like laughing wildly, times when he felt like crying. He wondered if this was what had shaped what he had become: serious, driven, self-absorbed (he now realised) – incapable of love?

In the end Raymond decided that he now knew why Miss Lillian had had such a powerful effect on him at Daphne Shepherd's tea party. There was a *personal* reason, after all. He felt very close to the woman from his father's past, which was also, for the first time, his own past, he now realised. He felt closer to his father than he had ever felt before. As a child he was always resentfully aware that he was considered a 'mummy's boy', relying on her for his sense of security; depending on her approval or censure to shape his response to the world. As a fatherless teenager, however, he had rebelled against her, and proceeded to construct what he has always considered his 'own' self. Since he was fifteen he had belonged to nobody.

Now he could discern the unacknowledged hand of his father in the shape of his world. His father had turned to Miss Lillian for passion; he, who had never known passion, felt it beginning to stir within him as he thought of Miss Lillian. Perhaps she might be able to release him from what he now, for the first time, considered to be a self-made prison — as she had done for his father.

Miss Lillian became an obsession. It did not interfere with his work or his routine, but his life — his mental life — expanded to include this new longing. He would meet her again, but not immediately, not until he was ready. He had first to savour her in memory and from afar. Raymond Rose did not stalk Lillian de Cunha; he knew better than that; but he arranged it so that he managed to see her often, in the distance, innocently, without having to go out of his way. Each time he saw her his longing increased. Eventually he started to write her a letter. He started many times, but couldn't get it right. Then, after a sleepless night, he got out of bed early one morning and wrote her a poem:

A LOVESONG FOR MISS LILLIAN

In the pulverised dawn
after sleepless nights
I find at the open window
the morning air charged
with the subtlest fragrances
that are signatures of you.

This is the gift of memory, perhaps,
(mine, and that of another before me)

memory strong enough to spark
the foolish riot of my blood;
and yet, how memory's power slips
and falls when the flesh is sad, needing
the touch of a warm hand, the nape
of a new world against my lips.

So I set forth in this paper boat
stirring the cold spaces between us,
as though paddling towards a star
down a reluctant, unfamiliar reach
of my life's river, hoping to harbour
in the calm certainty of your love.

He reread it every morning for a week, refusing to
alter or revise it in any way. Then he typed it, put it in a
plain envelope and mailed it to her – anonymously.

*

Like most people in their late fifties who live alone,
Liliana de Cunha was keenly aware of the process of
ageing. 'I am getting old,' she was always writing in
letters to her daughter and the many overseas friends
with whom she corresponded. Her constant letter
writing, she recognised, was an attempt to devour the
drift of time and the pain of distance and loneliness.
But Liliana had another recourse: she had long relied
on a friend, a professional fortune-teller in the
Amazon city of Manaus, to ensure that she was not
ambushed by the future and its unexpected terrors.
Lenor Araujo, her friend, worked with photographs:

her distant clients would send her a recent photograph of themselves (and twenty American dollars) and she would send back, in a week or two, a 'reading' of what the future held – usually in a single typed page.

Every year Liliana de Cunha obtained such a reading of her future. She considered it a prudent and necessary investment to safeguard her from the unexpected. She considered that Lenor had served her well over the years, having forewarned her about a car accident nearly ten years ago – she had not driven since that warning; Lenor had also predicted the acquisition of her home in Bel Air Park, the emigration of her daughter Tara to New York, and the unexpected demise of Sir Eustace Clarke, a leftover expatriate from colonial days who was until then her principal client and source of income. Her fortune-telling friend's only notable lapse was her failure, over five years ago, to predict the burglary of her home. It was her most unpleasant experience in all her years in Georgetown. She woke one night to discover a man in her bedroom, emptying her jewellery-case. He waved a gun at her and said that if she moved or opened her mouth he would kill her. He tied and gagged her before he left with what he wanted. The very next day she had written to Lenor, complaining that she should have been forewarned. She also immediately acquired a golden retriever and had him trained as her watchdog and companion in the house. She called the dog Samson, one of the names of Guyana's president, which she hoped would imbue the creature with sufficient authority and menace to enable it to protect her property and person.

A few days before Liliana turned up in the middle of Daphne Shepherd's tea party, she had received her annual 'reading' from Lenor. As well as translating them from Portuguese, these letters had to be 'interpreted'. She had to make sense of what the fortune-teller wrote in terms of her current circumstances. The letter seemed to contain one specific prognostication that filled her with dismay: her home was going to be burgled again – or at least there was going to be an attempt: '…another man will force his way into your home…' was her translation of the operative sentence from Lenor's letter. At first Liliana wondered if this could be a mistake, but she reasoned that, having made all that fuss about her lapse the first time, Lenor would have been very careful to get it right this time. But would not Samson, who was always in the house, warn her if anyone tried to get in? And what about all her new locks and bolts and wrought-iron protection at the windows?

Here was something else to add to the worries of her old age. She was also worried about money. Her daughter sent her something every month from New York – in addition to the occasional barrel of foodstuffs and other goods – but, although she was grateful, she was not comfortable with the idea of living off her daughter. A few kind gentlemen from her past sent her gifts of cash from time to time, but her major source of income, several thousands of dollars a month, could not be guaranteed for much longer. It came from the last (she told herself) of her big clients, Mr Matthew Anderson, who had founded a rum-distilling business which he had owned and run for most of his life, until he was persuaded to sell it at the age of seventy.

Never having married, Matteo, as Liliana called him in private, lived in a small apartment beneath the house of his niece, Babsie, who looked after the old man and his finances. Liliana had been for years his only source of carnal pleasure — indeed probably his only source of pleasure. He had arranged her monthly stipend fourteen years ago and had increased it several times over that period to keep pace with the slipping value of the currency. In recent years their assignations had diminished to a sad routine: Babsie would drop him at her house every Tuesday at noon: they would have a meal, with wine, followed by Liliana's famous crème brulée dessert, which he adored. The afternoon of 'lovemaking' that followed had become more and more farcical, as Matteo's aged body now refused to cooperate. Ever the perfect courtesan, Liliana had become gentle and solicitous — where in the past she had been teasing and provocative — and he grew to be quite satisfied with her tender, but inconclusive fondling. Always claiming that he had enjoyed himself immensely ('Just like the old days, my love…just like the old days! God bless you…'), he would have her phone for Babsie at six o'clock.

One Tuesday afternoon, a few months before Liliana had heard from Lenor about the impending burglary, she had left Matteo sitting in the living room as she retreated to the kitchen to put the finishing touches to their meal. For the previous three weeks nothing physical had occurred between them; they just sat close and talked. He would sometimes stroke her hair, or touch the outline of her breast. This Tuesday, however, when she re-entered the living room she found Matteo naked, his clothes scattered about the room, a strange look in his eyes. Samson was eying him enquiringly, his head tilted to one side.

'Oh dear, what have you done, Matteo? You've taken off all your clothes…'

His lips and tongue trembled as they always did these days when he prepared to speak: 'Getting ready,' he said, 'ready to do…the thing. Why don't you undress?'

'But my love, we haven't had lunch yet, aren't you hungry?'

'Lunch was lovely,' he said, puzzled, 'but Babsie will soon be here…We must do it now, or the children will find us…Besides, I'm all pumped up…' and he attempted a mischievous grin.

Liliana glanced down at the limp flag of his withered penis, slumped disconsolately against the inner thigh of his left leg, and could think of nothing to say. As she looked at his face she saw the long string of dribble that hung from his trembling lower lip. She saw, as if for the first time, the profusion of large, dark-brown moles and other discolourations on the light-brown and drooping skin of his face and on his fitfully heaving chest. His hands shook as he clutched the handles of the armchair and his right foot twitched, the toenails thick and grey. On his left foot he still wore a fawn-coloured sock, rolled down to the heel. Liliana suddenly glimpsed, as she looked at him, a reflection on her own life to come: its fragility and shame, the graceless attenuation of beauty, of physical capacity, of hope... She wept for her life, for her loneliness, then she called Babsie.

'I will miss the allowance,' she whispered to Babsie, as the two women helped him down the stairs, 'but I don't think you should bring him here any more; it's not fair to him. I blame myself for not realising it sooner.'

'Don't blame yourself, Miss Lillian,' Babsie said loudly, oblivious to the old man's presence. 'I know you've been very kind to Uncle Matthew. In fact I think you're the only reason he's still alive. These days he doesn't really know Tuesday from Thursday. If he ever asks, I'll say either that Tuesday has just passed or is still a few days away; he won't be any the wiser. As for the money, that's handled by the bank through a debit advise memo, and will probably continue, at least for a while.'

Although she had continued to receive her stipend for the next two months, Liliana prepared anxiously for the day when the cheque would not arrive. And now there was warning of another burglar...She felt that her world was closing in on her. It was in the midst of these concerns that she had looked, on the evening of the tea party, into the face of Raymond Rose as she shook his hand. When she heard the name, and realised who he was, there was a momentary confusion as she saw again the face of his father, the only man that she had ever loved, as she had told herself and several of her closest correspondents – after he had died. She instantly realised how much the son resembled the father. She had also remembered the incident in the cemetery, when she foolishly

71

decided to say her own goodbye to Jeff Rose and couldn't wait until the next day. The boy, of course, would not remember all that.

Although she knew that she could probably still mount a campaign of seduction which would land her some new and rich client who would pay for the privilege and pleasure of her womanhood, Liliana shuddered at the idea. She had reached, she felt, retirement age. Until recently she'd dreamed of settling down with a man she loved to a life where *she* would be the one enjoying all of life's pleasures, instead of anxiously providing them for a fee. Now she felt doomed to the company of the old and decrepit, like Matteo, and she wondered if she should not accept her daughter's invitation to retire to New York and live with her in the new flat. She was accustomed to facing her problems head on; now she felt vulnerable, no longer in control.

She remembered the time, a few years ago, the year before the president died, when the people in the customs department were giving her a hard time. They took to charging her exorbitant amounts for the outfits of clothing and the few luxury items that her daughter sent her in barrels from New York. It was the time of the barrels: everyone received them from relatives abroad – it was the only way life could be made bearable in those days.

When she complained to her friends they had told her: 'You don't know what to do? Just offer the customs man a raise. It's only money they want; that's why they giving you a hard time.'

But Liliana could not bring herself to be involved in

bribery. When she could bear it no longer – seeing her friends import all kinds of expensive things without paying duty, while she paid through her nose for the most ordinary of items – she made an appointment to see the president. She had met him socially at cocktail parties and public functions and he seemed to know everything about her. In those days she, and everyone else in Georgetown, it seemed, enjoyed the excitement of her notoriety ('The deadly Miss Lillian: she can afflict your husband's heart – and a spot eighteen inches below it – from fifty paces...'). She was nevertheless surprised at how readily the president agreed to see her.

As she walked into his office, he neither looked up nor greeted her nor offered her a seat, but continued writing on a pad in front of him.

'I hear you named your dog after me.'

Liliana was taken completely by surprise and it took her a few seconds to recover. 'Samson is also a name in the Bible,' she said uneasily.

'Of course it is, my dear Miss Lillian,' said the president with a smile as he rose and shook her hand. 'Won't you have a seat and excuse my bad manners – I couldn't resist the temptation to tease you a little.'

Liliana put her hand on her chest and sighed, then she chuckled: 'I wondered if you were going to have me arrested,' she said. 'Forbes is too good a name for a dog and Linden I have never liked, so Samson seemed the least problematic.'

'Is he as handsome as me?' the president asked.

'I wouldn't go that far, although he can be quite intimidating when he wants to be.' She gave him a meaningful look. 'But I don't want to take too much of your time, and I'm here about something else altogether.'

Then she made her complaint about the customs officers, even mentioning the remedy her friends had recommended.

'You're quite right to refuse to break the law by offering bribes to government officers, my dear; you're far more likely to be arrested for that than for naming your dog after the president! But I don't think a woman like you should bother too much about a few sweaty customs clerks – one or two choice phrases from your lips and a withering look would surely put them in their place. Be your magnificent self, Miss Lillian, and don't let them upset you. I offer you Shakespeare's well-known words about another beautiful woman like yourself: Cleopatra. "Age cannot wither you, my dear, nor the *customs* stale your infinite variety: other women cloy the appetites they feed, but you make hungry where most you satisfy."'

'Oh!' Liliana exclaimed, 'I never expected to be so shamelessly flattered by my president! Shakespeare and all…Well! I'm sorry to have bothered you about this, but I do feel better now that I've unburdened myself.'

They chatted a minute or two longer and then he stood behind his desk and shook her hand again. As she was about to go through the door, she heard him say: 'You know, you should have named him Odo!' When she looked back he smiled and waved his hand dismissively to indicate that she need not respond.

At first Liliana doubted that her visit to the president had achieved anything, but every time she received a barrel after that, although it was opened and its contents prodded a bit, she was never charged a cent of duty. Such memories of her resourcefulness and ability to cope in the past she dredged up to buoy her spirit in the bleak present. But she was not always pessimistic and would cling to any positive signs in the world around her and distract herself with the foibles and humorous behaviour of people she met. She was, for instance, in buoyant mood one afternoon as she sat down to write a letter to her daughter, Tara.

My dearest Tara,

I must thank you again for the lovely dressing gown you sent me via Desmond's aunt, who returned on Sunday. She brought me your parcel on Monday night, along with the wonderful news about your new apartment. I'm glad you're doing so well, my dear.

I'm really writing, however, to fill you in on the latest that is happening to me down here. Would you believe that your mother, at her age, has received an anonymous love poem? I have copied it out for you on a separate sheet (enclosed). Isn't it charming? – even if a little obscure in parts. What do you make of it? It's certainly good for a laugh and I've put it up on my little notice-board in the hallway – to cheer me up when I'm feeling down.

The thing is, I think I know who wrote it. As you will remember, Professor Savoury at the university invites me every year to give a talk to her Latin American Literature class on the Brazilian poets. Well, I did it a couple of weeks ago and there was a shy and nervous student – quite cute really – who sat in the back paying rapt attention. When I was finished he was the only one to ask a question and was so nervous about it that I had to help him along. During the coffee after class he came up to me and managed to stammer out that he'd really enjoyed my 'lecture', as he called it. I felt so pleased that he should go to all that trouble to be nice to me that I did what was probably a foolish thing: I kissed him on the forehead. Of course the others 'Oooh-ed' loudly and he was mortified, poor boy, but Professor Savoury told me later that he was quite bright, and a bit of a poet himself, so I have no doubt it was he who wrote me the poem. Whatever, I'm flattered.

Anyway, my dear, I must go and prepare dinner for Samson and myself. Will write again soon…

But two weeks later Liliana found herself in low spirits. It had been raining a lot and she'd been stuck in the house for a few days. She was not bothered at first; she'd managed to take Samson for a brief walk most nights, using her umbrella. These days she tended to use Courtney, her taxi-man, very sparingly, as she was fearful of his monthly bill. On Thursday night, however, when she'd phoned her friend Alice Jardine to say that she would be thankful for a lift to town on Friday to do her weekly shopping, Alice had informed her that her husband and the two boys were taking the car, early Friday morning, to drive to the Corentyne for the weekend – something about horse-racing at Port Morant. Liliana resigned herself to having to postpone her shopping until the following week. There was enough in the house to feed herself – the only thing was poor Samson. He had eaten the last of his favourite dog food three nights ago and had grown tired of the rice and table scraps she had been feeding him. That Thursday night he had staged a hunger strike in protest. Liliana, fearing that Samson might become too weak to tackle the expected burglar (and this could explain how Lenor's prognostication was going to be fulfilled) decided that, come what may, she would have to get to a shop the following day to buy his bag of dog chow.

On Friday morning she found out by phone that there was a shop not far away, on Sheriff Street, that sold the brand of dog food she needed. She dressed and decided that she would walk over there when the rain eased up a bit, then she would phone Courtney from the shop to come and drive her home with the heavy bag. As it happened, rain fell heavily all morning and into the afternoon, and the only time it had seemed light enough to venture out was when she was in the middle of her lunch. Liliana looked around her spotless home – the dark, polished floor, the expensive drapes from New York, the mahogany dining table with matching chairs upholstered in dark leather, the glass-fronted china cabinet, all the ornaments, carefully dusted and arranged... What did it all mean, she wondered, on the verge of tears, if she could no longer do something as simple as go out to the shop. It looked to her more and more as though she would have to sell everything, as so many people in Georgetown had done, and go to New York and live with Tara.

It was not until four o'clock in the afternoon that she managed to get out of the house. The store was not far, but the rain, though light at that time, was steady, and the afternoon traffic on Sheriff Street was very heavy – she was splashed a few times by passing cars and cursed under her breath in Portuguese.

When she had made her purchase, she asked if she could use the phone to call her lift, but learnt that the phone in the shop did not work when it rained. She had to go upstairs into the owner's home above the shop to use the phone there. Courtney's wife informed her that he'd left twenty minutes ago to take someone to the airport (Why hadn't she let him know that she would need him this afternoon?). She then called Hassan, whom she had used occasionally, but nobody answered. Liliana decided right then that she would emigrate to New York.

Wishing she had bought the smaller bag of chow, she hefted her purchase and made her way onto the street. She had to stop after two minutes to open her umbrella as the drizzle became heavier. With her purse over her shoulder, umbrella in one hand and shopping bag in the other, she moved awkwardly along, comforting herself with the thought of how happy her daughter would be when she received the letter saying that she would join her. It was at this point that Raymond Rose spotted her as he was driving along in the opposite direction in his BMW.

Because of the traffic it took Raymond a few minutes to turn around, but he soon caught up with her, stopping as he drew alongside. By this time it was raining quite hard. Raymond lowered the passenger window and opened the door.

'Please get in, Miss Lillian,' he said; 'we can't have you walking around in the rain like this.'

Before she realized who it was, she was protesting that she was already wet and would make a mess in the car.

'Think nothing of it,' Raymond insisted, and Liliana gratefully climbed in. 'You remember me, I hope,' he said as she closed the door and turned to look at him.

'Oh,' she said, 'I hadn't realised – it's Mr Rose, isn't it?'

'Please call me Raymond,' he said. 'We met a while ago at Daphne Shepherd's tea party.'

'I remember very well,' she said, 'and I'm very grateful for the lift; you've rescued me from a good soaking.' She looked sideways at his profile as he negotiated the heavy traffic. She could not help reflecting wistfully on the youthful male confidence she saw in him, that so sharply contrasted with her own mood and circumstance. She told herself sadly that a man like Raymond was precisely what she had forfeited forever by choosing the life she had… To banish such gloomy regrets, she told Raymond how she came to be walking in the rain.

Raymond reached into his top pocket and took out a business card. 'Look,' he said, 'if you ever need transportation again, or anything else, just give me a call at the numbers on the card; if I'm not there someone will find me and give me the message. You shouldn't be walking the streets in this weather and, I think you should know,' he continued, in what seemed to Liliana a strange excess of kindness, 'there is *nothing* that I would not do for you.'

'Well, thank you very much, but I really couldn't make such a nuisance of myself...'

'I insist, and you must promise me,' he said, turning into her street and slowing as he approached her drive.

'Oh no,' Liliana said, 'you needn't have turned into the driveway...' and she wondered briefly how he knew where she lived. As he stopped in front of the gate and she reached, embarrassed and confused, to open the door, Raymond said, in a tone of authority: 'Stay there, Miss Lillian, it's still raining.'

'But I'm already wet...'

Raymond got out of the car and opened the gate. Somewhere beneath her embarrassed protests, Liliana recognised the possibility of luxuriating in such attention – in such a display of care and protection and mastery. She shook her head, as though to dislodge an unworthy thought, as Raymond drove the car under the house, right next to the enclosed stairway. 'Now,' he said, 'we can get out.'

'Oh surely, Mr Rose, you will permit me to manage on my own from here. You have been very kind and already done more than enough.'

'No, I will take your bag up for you – unless you feel uncomfortable about letting me into your house.'

Liliana felt a light-headed helplessness that made her want to laugh. She had no choice but to let him follow her up the stairs. As she halted on the top landing to fumble for her keys, she could hear his breathing behind her and she felt a sudden thrill of excitement and fear. She dismissed it as a kind of professional reflex, sprung from her years of physical transactions with men. She had become too sensitively attuned to male breath and bravado… As they entered the hallway, Liliana was surprised and horrified to see Samson throw himself playfully upon Raymond, his tail wagging wildly, his forepaws up on Raymond's waist. Raymond dismissed Liliana's profuse apologies and her scolding remarks to her dog. ('Honestly,' she told him, 'he's never done anything like this before.') He chose to take its behaviour as a good omen, although he told Liliana: 'He probably knows that it's a bag of his dog-food I'm carrying…'

Raymond slipped off his shoes and followed Liliana into the kitchen in his socks. Just before he entered the spotless kitchen, he noticed his poem pinned to a small notice-board – another happy omen.

'Well,' Liliana said, when he had deposited the bag on the counter, 'you have done all that you possibly could for me – far exceeding the requirements of kindness and chivalry: I thank you most sincerely and promise that I won't ever allow myself to be such a nuisance again.' She moved as if to see him to the door, but Raymond stood his ground.

'I'm sorry, is something the matter?' she asked nervously, feeling again that premonitory thrill of excitement mingled with fear.

'Aren't you going to invite me to spend the night?' Raymond asked simply.

She caught her breath sharply, refusing to look at him, afraid of what she might see in his face. 'Please,' she said, 'why do you make fun of an old woman. I still have some feelings, you know – and my pride…'

'I never make fun of anyone; least of all a woman like you,' he said, his voice tense.

She turned and looked sharply at him to see if he was mocking her, but on his handsome brown face, so reminiscent of his dear father's, she saw something as familiar as it was unexpected – an intense look of male sexual longing that took her breath away. Her heart pounded with excitement and she felt herself dissolving at the knees.

'Well, are you?' he asked again. Then a note of pleading crept into his voice: 'I know I practically forced my way into your home, but I cannot help the way I feel…'

'Oh,' she said weakly, almost in a whisper, 'do as you like.' As she turned away from him her thoughts were racing. What he had said about forcing his way into her home made her realise that she had misinterpreted Lenor's letter: *this* was what she meant – not another burglary – *this*, that she would never have dreamed of, never dared to hope for – *this*, the solution to all her problems, *this* was her future, and not the confines of a miserable flat in New York. As she thought of being consumed in the youthful energy of his perfect body, a shiver of anticipation seized her and she turned to face him with a smile.

Give Back My Book

Patricia Duncker

Everybody present at the first meeting of the Library Committee was famous for something.

Yvette was famous for her vegetable garden. She watered her green rows every second day with great care and ardour. She pumped up the water and let it run in carefully prepared channels walled with earth. She grew tomatoes the size of boars' balls. Her potatoes were renowned in the market and her haricots verts swayed, drugged with pleasure, in the summer wind. She dug the plot regularly in the winter months and strewed interesting masses of stinking dung upon the dark turned earth. Sometimes, in the spring, she could be seen marking out rows with a plank, as if precise measurements were essential to the drama of fertility.

Benoît was famous for his skill with machines. If the thing had broken beyond hope he could still repair it with ingenious sawn-off bolts, soldered plaques of light steel, an old fan belt from a wrecked car and lashings of engine oil. The only electrical gadget that had ever defeated him was my washing machine, which I had purchased in England. 'C'est le cerveau,' he said miserably, 'c'est mort.' He hated to admit that he was powerless; the only spare part that could persuade the drum to roll again reposed in a factory over a thousand miles away. We shared a Pastis on the terrace, then another, then a third. Then we slagged off the government, moaned about our taxes, loaded the dead machine onto the trailer and rolled away over the hills to a secret crevasse into which we and we alone have the right to hurl unwanted building waste, barrels, white plastic garden chairs, mattresses and dead washing machines. We watched it dismember itself against the dank walls of the ravine and observed the wrecked parts settle amidst decrepit tortured fridges, defunct stoves and shattered televisions, their screens forever cracked and blank. Benoît was famous for technical rescues, but he knew when the crevasse was the only solution.

Marie-Christine was famous for sex. She had beautiful eyes ringed with suggestive black eye-liner – and enormous looming breasts, on display in all weathers, only just stacked inside bright, tight tank tops with tiny straps. She shaved her armpits infrequently. These springing black hairs drove us all wild with obscene passions. Her father was Spanish; flamenco pounded in her blood. We heard it in her little block heels as we stood dazzled by her swirling knee-length skirt that clung, desperate, to her buttocks. Each buttock shook as she pranced into the bakery. No one could understand why she wanted to join the Library Committee. She didn't need to read; all she had to do was lounge against counters and cars, on sofas and sunbeds or against pillars in church doorways. At our fête du village everybody got drunk and propositioned her. She pushed us all languidly away, but to me she smiled slightly and said, 'Tu n'es pas un garçon, ma chérie, t'es une fille?' The verdict was still no.

Jacqueline was famous for her sand paintings. She stripped and planed large planks of oak, prepared the base with varnish so that the wood did not suck up the oil paint, then added a layer of glue. The surface remained tacky to the touch for days. When it was quite dry she used a pale wash, several coats, and the wood gleamed ghostly in her studio. Then she began to work. She mixed sand with paint, gritty and disgusting to touch, but the surface was transformed, as if the wood had begun to sing. The sand swirled in great downward strokes, red, ochre, gold.

'When are you going back to England?' she asked, pensive, intent. 'I desire a jar of black sand.'

And so I scoured the English coasts for black beaches, wandered desolate across northern banks of sliding pebbles, hunting for the black sand of the cold seas, the sand that gave no pleasure and withheld its secrets. I came home triumphant, bearing three pickle jars of glittering black sand.

Those paintings were the centrepieces in her exhibition at Montpellier. They sold for thousands of euros. I took Yvette to the exhibition.

'I can see that they're good,' remarked Yvette as we peered at Jacqueline's unlikely titles: Sérénité, Création, and L'Origine du Monde, 'but they're not my thing at all.'

I was famous for being English. Being English is a habitable identity, all on its own. I was famous for being born elsewhere, for being foreign. I loved being English. The village issued me with a licence to be irresponsible, to absent myself from time to time, to live on an invisible, unearned income and to sit up late every evening, with the shutters open and the lights blazing, as if I had nothing to hide. Everyone teased me about my national pastimes: tea with milk, warm beer, foxhunting and the Queen. Foxhunting intrigued them most; not why we wanted to ban it, but why on earth we ever did it in the first place. An evil rumour did the rounds: I possessed a secret recipe for fox. This was hotly denied by all the members of the Library Committee, who knew for a fact that I was hopeless in the kitchen. I am a practising Catholic – to say believing would be going a little far – and this confused everybody. The English are all Protestants, aren't they? But I had purchased a large glowing statue of the Virgin Mary, picked out from an Irish shop selling religious equipment, and installed the lurid cast in a garden grotto, covered with shells. At Christmas I decorated it with flashing fairy lights. Everyone said, 'Ahhhhhh, how beautiful!' and went away, shaking their heads. I was voted onto the Library Committee to be in charge of foreign books, that is, every language that isn't French.

And so there were five of us that winter evening, sitting round a white plastic garden table, making do with bulging slatted chairs. We were there to make decisions. Who is going to apply for a department grant? Who will inform Monsieur le Maire of our desire to set up a library in the first place? When will we approach the Conseil Général? How will we staff the Library? How often would we be open? Then we tackled the really difficult questions. How many books could a full member take out? Did children pay a special rate? After all, we want them to read. Could the numerous holidaymakers be full members or could they pay a special, temporary membership fee? I wanted us to be linked up to the Internet and hold the catalogue online. Everyone else looked doubtful.

'We have to be online,' I declared, 'if we're planning to go truly international. And we must have a website to advertise our Muscat.'

The concept of international advertising carried the day. We all began to dream about becoming even more famous and possibly very wealthy. Our tiny library would become a nerve centre for the Muscat industry. Streets in the village would be named after us. We would be remembered forever. Yvette noted in the Minutes that we needed an extra telephone point for the new computer and a socket for the laser printer. She added 800 euros onto the wish-list budget to pay for the website. We sauntered home that night, magnificent, united, optimistic. A new era had begun.

One thing I have learned about being an ex-pat: you must never ask another ex-pat what they did before becoming a professional foreigner. Otherwise, you may as well say what the hell are you doing here, sound very rude indeed and have done with it. I just say that I used to be in business and took early retirement. And 'business' sounds dead boring, so no one asks any further. Anyway, the Midi is full of drunk, mindless, ex-business types who cashed up and cleared out. I don't appear at all odd. But I do have a past, a most interesting past. I brood about it every night. Here is the story of how I went into business and made more money than you could ever imagine.

In the early 1980s I was a passionate Socialist. I know, it sounds exceedingly strange now, like confessing to genital warts or chronic psoriasis. But I believed in justice, freedom, the equal distribution of wealth and a better life for all of us. I attended a summer school in Marseilles, run by the Communist University of the Future and it was there that I met Hassan.

I caught his eye across a crowded room.

The seminar was about Althusser and Psychoanalysis. Did transference take place in our relationship to whatever ISA was dominant in our lives? ISAs – for those of you who aren't Marxists – means Ideological State Apparatus. We're all surrounded by them, School, The Family, Universities. So far, so good. Were we infantilised by an oppressive love object, which devoured our affections? In my case I suppose that means the Church. I worked for Proctor and Gamble in the marketing department, and as I loathed work it didn't seem like an oppressive love object. I had clearly never achieved total transference. The discussion bordered on the insane. I crept out, looking shifty, and found Hassan smoking a cigarette in a gentle breeze on the steps.

'It's total shit, isn't it?'

'Yup.'

'What's your name?'

I told him.

'I'm Hassan. Come and have a pizza.'

We chomped our way through mozzarella and

pepperoni, then moved to the bar next door. We liked each other. It was an auspicious beginning. I know what you're going to ask me. Did I go to bed with him? No, I never went to bed with Hassan. We didn't have that kind of relationship; more's the pity. We were a bit jazzed up on cold beer and city heat. The asphalt was melting and we could hardly hear ourselves above the roar of the cicadas when Hassan asked me this:

'What is it that you most desire?'

My answer was unhesitating.

'To be very, very rich.'

'OK. I know only two ways of earning unimaginable sums of money without any intellectual effort whatsoever: selling phoney religions to white Westerners, or stealing cars.'

'The first choice is out, Hassan. I'm a believer.'

He bowed. 'The cars, then?'

I thought he was joking.

But this is how the business worked. Hassan never employed anyone to whom he wasn't intimately related. He came from a small village on the northern Iraq border; his family made a dash for it when Saddam Hussein's troops sacked and burned the village on the next hill. His whole family was in exile, housed in different Western cities. There were dozens of them; Hassan was one of fourteen children. That makes for a lot of cousins. He ran the whole thing like Al-Qaeda, with one exception. He also employed his sisters and they were part of the command structures. Indeed, the women were extremely powerful, his eldest sister was his right-hand man. We were one big family firm, no weak links and a lot of tribal loyalty. I was the frontwoman; white, English, educated, plausible. I had the perfect profile. My marketing experience came in very handy; so did my IBM systems training. I set up the public front of the firm. We raised money from the EU and various Western development charities to purchase our first batch of specialist agricultural equipment, subsequently despatched to the Third World. FARMING THE FUTURE evolved into a limited company, commercial, profit making yet with a humane, idealistic streak. We donated pumps for clean water and sold organic ploughs. The paperwork was impeccable. The accounts were in order. The VAT forms were done on time. But beneath the mask we wore another face: we were car thieves.

Luxury cars – Mercedes, Audis, BMWs – vanished from the car parks, streets and driveways, even from the very garages of the big rich cities: Berlin, Munich, London, Paris, Lyons, Nice, Genoa, Milan, Rome, Leeds, Manchester, Edinburgh, Barcelona and Madrid. We stripped them down, shipped them out, gave them new identities and then sold them on to posh African dictators or bandits in Uzbekistan who were fed up with Russian jeeps and dilapidated camels. We even delivered to terrorist organisations that were working on their image and wanted to look respectable. Wherever a coup occurred our orders doubled, and we had a whole raft of fresh clients. We also had rich protectors. We needed them; the bribes were just another form of VAT. Sometimes FARMING THE FUTURE clients required all our services, tractors, ploughs, deep bore pumps, solar-powered windmills, and blacked-out gorgeous stretch limousines; but we never confused the two modes of operation. So I often found myself negotiating two rather different deals with the same Ministers of State, in the beginning via special courier and latterly through different websites, without their knowledge of the facts.

Our Head Office was based in Istanbul. This is the city where East and West shake hands before agreeing to go their separate ways. We planned for catastrophe; a rapid route out to Northern Iraq through Turkey existed in a sequence of family cars and safe houses. We might, at any moment, be investigated, rumbled and betrayed. Our exit time was two hours. The European networks operated quite separately from each other. Sometimes, as a safety precaution, we had to shut down an operation in progress – let one of the networks go cold for a year or so. The other groups took up the slack. Nearly all our business was conducted in code via the telephone. What could be more natural than a sister in Madrid ringing her younger brother in Berlin and asking him what he was eating, then insisting, in a matronly way, that he eat something different, something better for his stomach. Sending each other regular money was a normal, supportive family thing to do. So was saving for disaster and retirement. We were invisible to the outside world.

But we weren't the Robin Hoods of Istanbul. I have to be honest about that. We were lining our own pockets, or rather our offshore accounts. To put it bluntly, we were crooks. Up-market gentleman crooks, the best sort. But we weren't doing it for fun, we were making buckets of money. When people asked him where we had met Hassan always told the truth.

'We met at the Communist University of the Future. We believe in the future,' he added fervently. Our future, nobody else's.

Hassan's eldest sister was very beautiful. She didn't much like me. She thought that I was the reason Hassan never married. I didn't think I was. We were friends – close, intimate friends. But we were both afraid that bedroom scenes might disturb the seamless harmony of the office. So we concentrated on running the company and making money. Sometimes we found ourselves involved in those significant, but unfinished conversations that you have from time to time with a beloved colleague.

'Do you ever wish that things could have been different between us?'

'Mmmmm? Yes, I do.'

Then one of us would say, 'Maybe one day. Maybe soon.'

But the promise of 'soon' wasn't just around the corner. I had a flat in Istanbul that was owned by Hassan's uncle, a sleeping partner in the firm. When the uncle manifested an untoward interest in me Hassan nearly decked him. They had words, strong words, and I received a written apology for the insult that had been perpetrated against my honour. My honour, I ask you. The uncle had only suggested a quiet dinner somewhere well lit and expensive. But I was very pleased about the incident. Hassan cared. He cared about me! But Hassan's sister wasn't pleased. She rang up and accused him of sleeping with me in secret and then lying about the whole affair. I sent her a gift crate of tea and goodies from Fortnum and Mason and she calmed down. However, the incident with the lecherous uncle confirmed one thing. Hassan regarded me as his private property; whether or not he decided to take possession was up to him.

We worked together from 1 July 1986 until 23 September 2002 and then we saw the red light, full on. We were outwitted by new technology and the German police. One of the cars was fitted with a tracking device we had never encountered before, hadn't detected and couldn't disable. The luscious new Mercedes, with enhanced acceleration, the latest satellite navigation equipment, leather seats, walnut dashboard, drinks cabinet and computer-assisted steering, left the street outside the racetrack at Baden-Baden one night, and was thoroughly done over before leaving the country on one of our transports. The dream car passed peacefully through Austria and Italy before suddenly becoming live and glowing in the hold of a Greek-registered cargo ship in the middle of the Mediterranean. We rechecked the vehicles when they landed, of course we did. But Interpol was waiting with us on the quay as our last shipment of easy wealth floated home.

I think it helped that Hassan speaks beautiful English and is obviously wealthy and educated. He promised to cooperate fully with the police and help track down the criminals who were exploiting FARMING THE FUTURE for their own benefit. He introduced me as his lovely, English wife. I rang his eldest sister and told her the whole story in horrified tones, knowing full well that the call was being monitored and recorded. Operation Meltdown went into execution. We'd had sixteen good years. Time to fold our tents and head off to another part of the desert.

Our getaway identities changed from time to time over the years, but when the moment of disaster struck I found myself in a small isolated village in the South of France with no swimming pool and a chimney that smoked. Hassan vanished back into Iraq, which was instantly invaded by America. This turn of affairs proved to be exceedingly useful. The family, jubilant, regrouped upon their abandoned mountain, for what could be more natural than the western exiles coming home, to set about rebuilding their nation in a flurry of wealth and optimism. Not one of them was tactless enough to drive back in a Mercedes although some high quality Land Rovers, top of the range, with reinforced bull bars, did slide quietly over the border. Hassan's troops were disciplined, intelligent, calculating. Ostentatious wealth was out: no Rolex watches or iPods. But a dozen little businesses, backed by solid capital, suddenly sprang up and flourished in the wilderness. I was left dealing with a new life on my own, managing the finance, and unable to touch my offshore accounts.

'Don't ring the mobile, except in emergencies, and never ring the standing line,' advised Hassan. 'I'll keep in touch via Special Courier.'

And to be fair he did. I didn't lack for anything at all. My exceedingly generous allowance was only a proportion of the interest accruing on my capital. One part of the funds in Switzerland allowed instant access, and I received long loving letters from the now middle-aged man who had once enchanted me, twenty years ago, in a bar in Marseilles. We no longer had any daily business to discuss, and so Hassan concentrated upon love. He had always adored me, and now he was free to speak, to tell me that I had grown more beautiful with every year, how my full figure ravished his dreams and how his passion waxed with the enlarging moon. He also claimed that his eldest sister longed to embrace me, and to greet me as a sister of her own. This was of course a code for discussing the situation of the accounts and the investment placements, but he wrote with such flourishes of conviction that I found myself reading the letters twice, first for the financial instructions buried therein, and secondly for sentiment.

My Love, My Treasure, My Life's Work,
When I look upon your tender handwriting *(the Swiss account)* and dream of our last meeting in the mountains *(confirmation that I do mean the Swiss account)* I feel my heart turn over *(the interest rates have gone up)* and my passion for you blooms without limits. *(Large increase in the rate of the high interest deposit!)* I can no longer live without seeing you *(transfer the money from Jersey to Switzerland)*, and I dream that I shall kiss all your fingers and then all your toes. *(Not all the money, just the interest accrued over ten months.)* The scent of your body haunts my

waking hours; I would cross oceans of time to be with you, yet I cannot touch you. *(Don't interfere with the American money.)* You are imprinted forever upon the secret places of my heart *(Eh?? that doesn't mean anything)*; you are my rising up and my lying down, *(that doesn't either)*, I feel your breath and no other present in the wind *(the police aren't onto us)*, yet you are so distant, *(don't ring)*, – I beg you, reach out a hand to me. *(Write.)* Be gracious as you always are – *(usual Special Courier)* – and tell me that you long for my mouth upon your body *(let me know when you've completed the Swiss transactions)*, my lips upon your nipples. *(Hassan! You're losing it)* Your sweet weight against my chest *(your allowance will be paid as usual)* is all that I desire, imagine our ecstatic reunion, our writhing arms, our mouths soldered together. *(Writhing? soldered? I keep forgetting that Hassan never studied literature. He graduated in Accountancy and Business Studies.)* My Sweetest Love. You are always in my mind,

Hannibal

(Hassan was a long term Tom Harris fan)

Meanwhile, back in the Midi, I was famous for being English. But I was lonely and bored. I dedicated myself to religion and the Library Committee. I counted the days until the arrival of the next Special Courier.

Suddenly the Maire gave Yvette the green light. Our proposals and applications had been held up by strikes in the Préfecture, and lain gathering grit on an abandoned desk in the increasing heat. But now the strikes were settled, the money forthcoming, the project underway. We called an emergency meeting round the picnic table in the old school room that would one day be our Library, and gazed with pleasure at the new telephone point, already in the wall. We produced a packet of pistachios, another of mixed nuts, and sliced a small roll of salami into fine portions; then we opened a cool box with the Pastis and Muscat nestling in ice. We unwrapped a box of chocolates, congratulated ourselves, and prepared to celebrate. After a long and amiable argument about what to call the Library we decided upon the title: Bibliothèque Municipale.

Then, just as dusk crept over the garrigue, the door flew open and a small man with a white beard and rimless round glasses marched in and made a startling announcement.

'Excusez-moi pour le retard. I am Professor Büchner, and I wish to join the Library Committee.'

We all gazed at him, speechless, appalled. No one simply joined the Library Committee; you had to be chosen. He spoke passable French with a terrible accent. I was the only person there who didn't know who he was. The retired Professor from Tübingen moved down to the Midi for the sake of his weak chest. He owned an even smaller wife and a very elderly German shepherd with a white muzzle who now lay upon the tiles, gasping. Benoît had installed all his kitchen plumbing and his – C'est bien, c'est beau, c'est Bosch — cooker, fridge, freezer, dishwasher and washing machine. He bought one of Jacqueline's sand paintings at the Montpellier exhibition: 3,000 euros. She studied him rapaciously. He purchased courgettes and aubergines from Yvette at the market and then placed a regular home delivery order; he had even given Marie-Christine the eye in the Post Office. Now he sat down amongst us and helped himself to a handful of nuts. Yvette recovered herself.

'I'm very sorry, Monsieur. We are holding a meeting.'

'I know. That's why I came.'

It sounded very churlish to say we had no intention of extending the membership.

I bubbled with rage; Professor Büchner was clearly famous for being foreign, and had almost certainly emerged from a glorious academic career of prestigious lectures and honorary degrees, a past he had no need to conceal.

'Where are the books?' He snaffled a chocolate.

We gaped.

'We can't order them until our application is given the final go-ahead by the Préfecture,' Benoît explained. He didn't find the Professor especially intimidating, as the man knew nothing whatsoever about machines. We had already liquidated the Muscat, so Jacqueline offered him a Pastis. He accepted graciously.

'Everyone has books they don't want,' said the Professor. 'Let's send a leaflet round the commune and have a Deliver Your Books to the Library Day. Like an amnesty for guns. That method always yields treasures. As well as a lot of crime novels.'

Yvette liked the idea. Why hadn't we thought of it before? She offered the Professor another chocolate.

SUPPORT YOUR BIBLIOTHEQUE MUNICIPALE
ALL BOOKS GRATEFULLY RECEIVED
READ IT? DON'T BIN IT!
BRING IT ROUND TO YOUR NEW LIBRARY
TUESDAYS & THURSDAYS 6-8 PM
Vivez mieux – un livre par semaine!

'That should do the trick,' declared the Professor. He looked crafty and cheerful. We salaciously anticipated an influx of erotic crime novels.

I was sitting at the picnic table, sorting through an unstable pile of books and placing them in orderly rows, spines to the front: local history, cookery, a surprising collection of Westerns with hatchet-faced cowboys wielding lassoes, every known genre of romantic fiction and kilometres of crime – when Gilles Deroux crept into the Library. The Professor was sitting beside me, deep in Zane Grey's *Riders of the Purple Sage*, translated into German. He handed over the dreadful process of final catalogue decisions to me; but this involved reading enough of each book to decide what it was and where it should be placed. I was studying *Grands Vins de France*, which described both the landscape and the grapes. Does it belong under Travel writing or National vineyards?

'Bonsoir Madame, Monsieur.' Gilles, otherwise dubbed the Village Idiot, and famous for surviving his mother's rule, shuffled forward, uncomfortable and insidious. He was carrying a large, tatty, battered book with a nineteenth-century binding and faded gold letters on the cover. The markings on the spine were entirely obliterated. He laid it down before us on the table.

'Thank you, Gilles. This certainly looks like an antique.'

The Professor nodded at Gilles and I opened the book. Here were pictures, some beautifully coloured, of rocks, precious stones, obscure plants, and strange symbols, triangles and hexagons, patterns of numbers, phases of the moon, carefully calculated, strange poems in code. Some of it looked like recipes. The main text was written in Latin.

'I don't know if many people in the village will be able to read this Gilles.'

'My mother can read it,' said Gilles defensively.

'Let's have a look.' The Professor took the book from my hands and was as immediately engrossed, as he had been in the Western.

Gilles Deroux lived with his mother in a remote farmhouse with no electricity or running water, which still sported an outside lavatory. She harboured a dozen goats, a reputation as a crack shot, and proved intolerant of strangers. I knocked on her door once to say hello when I was walking in the hills. I never did it again. A huge red-faced woman with lumpy floral breasts bulged out of the door and yelled, 'Que voulez-vous, Madame?' directly into my face. I apologised for my existence and slunk off, never to return.

'And how is your mother, Gilles? Is the stream low up at Salsis?'

No one knew how the two of them managed for water, but Madame Deroux had been seen with a large blue barrel wedged in the back of her truck.

'Comme toujours,' said Gilles.

The Professor looked up. 'You can't give us this. It ought to be in a museum. It's a medieval Grimoire.'

At the next Library Catalogue meeting the Professor burbled with deranged excitement over *The Book of Spells* – an early eleventh-century collection, probably based on Egyptian sources. We must have the thing valued, restored, rebound. Gilles and his mother are throwing away millions of euros. We can't let them do this. Where did it come from? How did they get hold of this thing? We summoned Gilles, who had been seen in the forecourt at the Cooperative. But there were no answers to any of these questions and Gilles appeared very anxious to donate the book. He banged off back up the mountain and would take no part in any further discussions concerning its future.

Meanwhile Professor Büchner worked himself up into an intellectual fit.

'This Grimoire is priceless! Its discovery is an event of immense historical significance!' he thundered.

'Will we be on the local TV news?' Marie-Christine adjusted her bra strap.

'Should we ring the Beaux-Arts?' asked Jacqueline.

'Shall I make a box for it?' suggested Benoît, anxious to be helpful.

'Will it get stolen?' Yvette worried about security.

'Can anybody read Latin?' I had yet to be convinced of its usefulness.

'I can,' snapped Professor Büchner.

'All right then. Read out some useful spells.'

This came out as a challenge. But I was really worrying whether I should catalogue the Book under gardening or cookery. The Professor retired into a corner and caressed each page of the Grimoire for more than an hour. We continued to organise our hybrid collection and resumed our chatter. Suddenly the Professor lit up, reactivated.

'Here's one for you, Yvette. How to triple the yield of your garden.'

Yvette roared with laughter. We joined in.

'More manure!'

'Fertiliser!'

'Piss on it!'

'No. It sounds quite scientific. Wait for the night of the sickle moon. Then mix the following libation, which must be poured into the earth, accompanied by this prayer. I can do a translation if you like.'

'Then it should be catalogued under gardening,' I sang out, triumphant. I filled out an entry for *The Book of Spells*. Yvette wrote down the Professor's ad hoc translation, but was bewildered by some of the ingredients.

'Where do you imagine I'm going to get three cupfuls of ground camel dung?'

'The Zoo at Montpellier?'

'It's too complicated.'

'The English at Pardailhan! They've got llamas. Aren't llamas related to camels?'

We flung ourselves into solving the mysterious puzzles presented by this unique combination of ancient Egypt and medieval France. After all, if it worked we would be the beneficiaries. We might even be able to patent the mixture, like the monks in the Grand Chartreuse.

'Just think,' said Marie-Christine, dreamily, 'giant tomatoes.'

'There's a recipe for love potions here,' said the Professor, ogling the next page, 'and one on how to make men impotent.'

'I don't want men to be impotent.' Marie-Christine glowed suggestively, and we became very thoughtful.

Well, we all got involved in chasing up the ingredients for Yvette's spell. We learned the prayer by heart and rehearsed the chant at every meeting, like a team song. We waited for the dark of the moon.

'Must be something in it,' said Benoît. 'My father says you should always plant with the rising moon.'

But it was June in a rainy year and the gardens were in full swing, bursting with promise and blossom. It was hard to see how nature's power could be bettered. By the time the fatal night arrived we had filched barrowloads of llama dung and changed dozens of bottles of wine into vinegar, preparing, practising. We had five times the amount of magical concoction required by the Grimoire.

'May as well chuck it all on,' Yvette decided.

'Is that wise?' I was always the cautious one. 'Won't it kill the lettuces? Vinegar can't be good for lettuces.'

'It'll kill the slugs,' said Jacqueline.

We chanted the prayer over our aperitif, the Professor beating time on the arm of his chair. We exploded into giggles and he accused us of not taking the whole thing seriously. The Grimoire lay open before us, supported on its new portable wooden lectern, constructed by Benoît; for this was our Bible, our guide through the New World of wealth and power promised in its pages. We had all gone slightly mad. We were having a wonderful time.

At ten o'clock in the closing dusk Yvette led the way across her gardens. We carried candles in jars and Marie-Christine was wearing a long dark cloak to enhance the atmosphere. Had we been seen? What would the village think? God knows. We were sufficiently drunk not to care. Round and round the grassy path we went, circling the garden, chanting softly, repeating the prayer seven times, as required by *The Book of Spells*. Then we stood still, holding our breath as Yvette moved silently between her gorgeous flowering rows, pouring the evil-smelling liquid into the earth. She was a priestess, conjuring the seeds to fruition. We shivered, excited, impressed, and strangely on edge.

Would it work?

Time to retire to the kitchen and our seafood casserole with the flaming gambas.

Over the following weeks we badgered Yvette for information. How were the aubergines? Were the onions any bigger? What about the melons over the wall by the river? Everything looked magnificent. But no larger than usual. We sank back into our usual activities, ordered the shelves for the Library and continued to catalogue the mounting pile of books. I began to look out for the Special Courier again. Professor Büchner kept the Grimoire at home and studied it in the evenings. The Book became his obsession; he was translating spells on the side. No one was prepared for what happened next.

Yvette turned up late for the first meeting in July. She rattled right up to the door in her blue van, white-faced and simmering with revelation.

'It's happened!' she cried, wrestling with a huge cardboard box on the passenger seat. 'Look at this!'

Yvette had climbed over the wall to check out her melons, anxious to murder the water rat that had chewed up the artichokes in her neighbour's garden. The rat lay dead and rotting upon a stone by the river and her melons had turned into gigantic green globes, the size of Chinese lanterns. Usually she got half a dozen or so by this time of year but now there were nearly thirty bulging fruit, voluptuous, vast, ripe, pressing against her feet, as if she had stepped into paradise.

'But that's not the worst of it.' Yvette's confession was unexpected. 'We made so much of that stuff when we got the second lot of llama dung I wasn't sure what to do with it. So once I had covered my garden I tipped it into the river.'

'You did what?'

Professor Büchner was suffering from a paroxysm; the spell had almost certainly entered the water table.

'Everyone else irrigates with water from the river. I pump up my water from an underground spring.'

'So?'

'The lotissements by the bridge.' Yvette was by now gasping with hysteria. 'No one knows what's happened. The potatoes are the size of land mines. Madame Chiffre has green beans as fat as your forearm!'

'Oh God!'

'Did anyone see us?'

'Then it's worked!'

We stared at one another, utterly horrified that what we most desired had come to pass. Professor Büchner was the first to pull himself together.

'But this is wonderful. The libation is clearly an ancient form of Egyptian fertiliser. It might have immense commercial potential.'

We all contemplated our futures as millionaires in agricultural chemicals. I would dig a swimming pool at once and have the smoking chimney reconstructed. Jacqueline saw herself as the director of her own art gallery. Marie-Christine gleamed at Benoît. She could set him up in his own electrical plumbing business. He was a good man, honest, faithful. Marriage and children materialised before her in appealing softened focus. She smiled into his face. He turned brick red.

'What other spells are there in this Book?' I demanded.

We told the Maire that we needed more time to prepare for the Library's opening festivities. We needed to redesign the logo and make up some more rules. We needed to meet twice a week. Indeed, we needed the entire summer to get it all exactly right. And so, intense and disciplined, like a crack medical research team about to discover a vaccine for all known diseases, we set about our work. We realised that we could improvise on the ingredients, but not on the proportions or the quantities. We needed time to work things out. We distributed copies of the Professor's translations. Some of the most promising spells required huge amounts of crushed insects. Jacqueline and I spent hours in the University Library in Montpellier, buried in the ancient Egyptian archaeological section, drawing scarabs and locusts and comparing them to cicadas and stag beetles. We were baffled by the nature of the magical demands: wealth, sons, good weather, magnificent harvests and victory over one's enemies all seemed standard practice in medieval witchcraft, but warding off the Evil Eye or increasing our numbers of slaves didn't seem to have much modern relevance. There was a very long section on how to produce floods and stop sandstorms, and a plethora of sinister embalming rituals.

Meanwhile Yvette's rivals in the market gardens were reaping the benefits of her improvidence in the river. Her own crop increased, but not as dramatically as the melons, which carried all before them. Everyone down in the lotissements spent hours marvelling at a summer miracle. For the extravaganza continued without let or hindrance: peaches, apricots, raspberries, gigantic, succulent, luscious. It was as if the goblin men had taken over the gardens. Come buy! Come buy! Would it ever wear off? The phenomenon neither slackened nor waned. The vineyards downstream became profligate in their abundance. We studied the course of the river. Eventually, the Cessenon joined the Aude and irrigated a valley full of maize fields. There was now no stopping whatever it was that we had unleashed. All this gave rise to some tardy ethical reflections. We shouldn't have quadrupled the quantities. What if the whole thing had been enhanced by the llama dung? How could we control this power which had come to us, unbidden?

Luckily, the Grimoire was locked up in Professor Büchner's drinks cabinet when Madame Deroux stalked through the door.

'You stole my Book,' she roared and a row of crime novels teetered over. 'I want my Book.' She pounded on the table.

'GIVE BACK MY BOOK!'

Yvette rose up to pacify her and was hurled back into her white plastic chair. No one dared to speak. Madame Deroux attacked the shelves. I noticed that she went straight to gardening rather than cookery, which meant that I had correctly catalogued the Grimoire.

'FIND MY BOOK!' she yelled.

'Dear Lady...' ventured the Professor. She felled him with a giant swing from her moist and scabby fist.

'You stinking piece of German filth!' she raged.

Madame Deroux was clearly going to wreck the joint and kill us all. I felt responsible. I had been the person who had accepted the Grimoire from Gilles, in good faith. I addressed the dragon from a safe distance.

'Madame! We had assumed that the Book was a donation. We are aware that it is extremely valuable and we have locked it away for safekeeping. We will have it back in your hands within three days.'

Madame Deroux glowered at me like a boar at bay. The Library Committee gasped, horrified. Give back the Book? Never! I knew this sounded like a unilateral declaration, but I hadn't given up stealing cars to become a book thief. And in any case, if we all clubbed together we could have the entire thing copied by the laser scanner in the Rare Books Service at the Montpellier University Library.

'But...' said Benoît.

'We think...' said Marie-Christine.

'That is to say...' interrupted Jacqueline.

'Madame, it is your Book,' I was unexpectedly seconded by the Professor who was still on the floor, but whose erudite authority dominated our decisions, 'and it will be returned to you.'

'You damn well see that it is,' shouted Madame Deroux, 'by Saturday night.'

She slammed the door behind her. A faint crack appeared in one of the glass squares. We stared at one another, guilty, shocked, appalled.

'Why on earth did you say we'd give it back, you idiots?' screeched Yvette, who had been planning a further experiment with the llama dung. I revealed my laser copying scam and the entire committee re-illuminated with satisfaction, except for the Professor. He was back on his chair nursing his chin. Benoît had gone to get some ice from the Café next door.

'It won't work,' the Professor said flatly. 'The Grimoire has to be present for the spells to take effect. It says so on the first page. The power resides in the Book itself. That's why we had it set up on the kitchen table when we mixed Yvette's fertiliser. I laid it on the wall when she went down to her melons. The Book was present when she chucked the remains into the river. If I had carried it round in the gardens Yvette's beans would now look like anti-tank missiles.'

'Why didn't you tell us?'

'You didn't need to know.'

'Then why did you say you'd give it back?' I actually spat at him. He set me straight.

'Well, you volunteered to return the Book to its owner. And we must give it back. It's the right thing to do.'

Benoît arrived with ice wrapped in a dishcloth. The Professor's jaw was dark red, becoming purple. He didn't look too good. We applied the lumpy wedge of ice.

'Doesn't the Book now belong to the Bibliothèque Municipale?' suggested Jacqueline.

'Listen,' said the Professor, 'we don't know who Madame Deroux really is. But I think she is the Keeper of the Book. It will therefore be safe in her hands. No one else can use the Book without risking terrible damage.'

'I bet she used it to control Gilles,' I said gloomily.

'She probably made him impotent,' said Marie-Christine.

'Camille Deroux is just a bad-tempered old cow who lives in the mountains,' snapped Yvette, 'and has a simple-minded son.'

During the three days that remained to us, we mourned the Book and its imminent loss. We also learned with alarm about the sudden burst of excessive fertility that had struck the maize fields of the Aude. Scientists from Montpellier were testing the water. The splendour of the valley made the TV news. Tourism increased, and the luminous beauty of Languedoc Roussillon was proclaimed the envy of the nation. Everywhere else the land was parched and dry, but upon our holy mountain the vines, olives, peaches and cherries grew prodigal and flourished.

Even the Professor, camped out upon the moral high ground, regretted the Grimoire. On the last night we sat together in the Library, turning the pages.

'Look, this is interesting,' he said, indicating a strange pentagram. 'It spells out a code. It can tell you what it is you most desire.'

'Only fools don't know what they want,' snapped Yvette.

Benoît and Marie-Christine were holding hands. Suddenly I realised that the Grimoire could grant one last service.

'I don't know what I most desire. I want to know. I'll do the spell.'

Everybody looked up, startled.

'Is that wise?' asked the Professor.

'Translate the spell.'

The Professor took up his pencil and applied himself to the Latin.

'You have to give me something that you care about passionately. An object. Something you love and touch and keep close to you.'

I didn't hesitate.

I produced my most recent letter from Hassan, which I carried in my jacket pocket, next to my heart. I spread it out flat upon the table. Everybody leaned over the much folded and unfolded paper. Hassan wrote in English, so they wouldn't have recognised the finer points and I hope no one understood the word 'nipples', but it was clearly a love letter. They all stared at me enraptured, saucer-eyed. Here was the Englishwoman's secret. Here was her hidden life, written, revealed. She had a lover.

'Is he really called Hannibal?' asked Marie-Christine. She never watched horror movies right through to the last lurid shot.

'No. It's a pseudonym.'

It took hours to make the code work. The mathematical formulae eluded Professor Büchner. We lost interest and went back to updating the catalogue and the gossip. Then the Professor called me over.

'Speak to the Book. Ask your question. I want to check something.'

'Speak to the Book?'

'Yes. Go on. I think any language will do.'

'OK.' I took a deep breath.

'Please tell me what it is I most desire.'

The Professor checked the Latin, spelt out from the code.

'Well, it says here that twenty years ago a man gave you what you most desired and that what you most desire now is that man.'

Ahhhhhh! A huge sentimental sigh escaped from the assembled Library Committee. The Englishwoman is in exile and separated from the one she loves. We all long to go home and be loved. You don't need a Grimoire to tell you that.

I ran straight back to the house with no swimming pool and a smoking chimney and rang Hassan's eldest sister on the mobile – the emergency signal.

'What's happened?' she screeched.

'Nothing. Get Hassan to ring me.'

Half an hour later I heard a beloved voice crackling with suppressed hysteria.

'What's wrong? Where are you?'

'Nothing. You know that flat we had in Istanbul?'

'What?'

'Is your uncle still in it?'

'No. It's rented out.'

'Evict the tenants and wait for me there. I'm coming home.'

'You're doing what?'

'Don't keep saying "what", you rotten bastard. I love you with all my heart and I'm coming home. You're home. Wherever you are – is home.'

There was a muffled pause; and then his voice rang out, all the way from the lost mountain villages of Northern Iraq. He sounded like a young man again, like a young man able to give me everything I could desire.

'My love at last! My love!'

'Send me the tickets,' I yelled.

This is how the story ends. Gilles Deroux rented my house and fixed the chimney. His mother recovered her Grimoire and then gave him the boot, so he was desperate for somewhere to live. Professor Büchner delivered the keynote address at the Library's opening fiesta. Everybody clapped like madmen, but I wished he hadn't used quite so many Latin quotations. We held an exhibition of Jacqueline's sand paintings, both in the Library itself and in the Café next door. She sold most of them and there was an article about her – 'La Reine des Sables' – in the *Midi Libre*. Marie-

Christine and Benoît were married in the autumn. They've moved into town, but she comes back every weekend to quarrel with her mother. I hear there's a baby on the way. Yvette installed a pipe into the river and now waters her garden directly from the Cessenon. Her aubergines swell to a magnitude I find grotesque and her lemons look like giant yellow hand grenades. The effects of the spell show no signs of abating. Our land is rich, verdant, moist, like the delta of the Nile. Our fruits fatten to the song of the cicadas, and our micro-climate has been officially attributed to global warming. But of course, none of us have confessed to anything.

Hassan and I do quite a bit of travelling. He has come to a satisfactory arrangement with the Americans, who are now officially in charge of our mountain top, and we shall be spending next winter in California. He says he'd rather deal with the Yanks as his business associates than as The Enemy. We can't decide which religion to adopt so we haven't married. This gets up his sister's nose. She still doesn't like me.

Hide And Seek

Aritha van Herk

In a previous life, Tip spent days with her fingers tap-dancing over a computer keyboard, producing reports of marketing conditions and spreadsheets of implacable numbers. This occupation, once defined as secretary and then more euphemistically and dangerously broadened to 'office assistant' was a banner of drudgery. She arranged and re-arranged words, columns of numbers that might or might not add up to some distant total, occasional black and white photographs of square buildings illustrating the content. But when Tip's friends asked her what Seaforth and Associates did, she was at a loss to explain. They seemed to have interests in frozen foods and their distribution, but that did not account for their sub-companies or their sidelines, which provided services as odd as installing and maintaining snack-dispensing vending machines, and an arm's-length branch specialising in the extermination of vermin or insects. They preferred to call that branch the pest control group. Although there was little evidence in the information she saw, Tip suspected that Seaforth merely administered a range of different services, all of them related to necessities like drinks bottles and mousetraps.

Still, Tip was herself surprised when she noticed how often she thought about not just changing her life but re-locating, escaping her own body and its identification. Disappearance is a temptation that only a few contemplate, the sheer dizzying nerve of such an act, to walk away one morning from domestic particulars and to step sideways into another life, possibly parallel but completely unconnected. Disappearing is the nirvana of those who mistrust their own intentions.

Of course, pulling off a disappearing act is difficult. When someone leaves without the customary conclusions or goodbyes, those who share the old life expect foul play. And once suspicion is aroused, the whole engine of overwrought attention follows: police, private detectives, extra-perceptive and curious observers who couldn't help but notice a particular woman with red hair driving a green car stopping for petrol off the A21. The busybodies of the world make a habit of observing what others wish to conceal, insist on noticing gestures and traces meant to be invisible. We are all passionately interested in 'foul play,' we all relish the unsavoury. Oh, most of us would never bloody a knife or cram another person's body into the boot of a car, but we are alert to treacherous behaviour, wonderfully interested in its performance, and gullible to the stagecraft that surrounds it. Foul play takes place at night or in the dark, it results in close scrutiny of torn scraps of paper, of habits that do not match with routines.

Tip's Ivan was an avid practitioner of the daily detective game. 'Look,' he'd say, nodding his head toward a couple walking down the pavement in front of them. 'They've had a fight.'

'How can you tell?'

'They're walking exactly nine inches apart. Too close to be strangers, but too far away to be happy together.'

Tip rolled her eyes to let him know that she mistrusted his analysis, but she found, to her own discomfiture, that he was relentlessly observant of such invisible communication, an eavesdropper in restaurants, a gimlet-eyed side-glancer on the Tube.

'Feet hurt?' he inquired, hanging his jacket on the coat rack.

'Why?'

'You left your shoes in a definite attitude of disgust at the door. You must have flung them off.'

'I was just in a hurry, Sherlock.'

But he would swallow a self-satisfied smile while Tip seethed inside. This microscopic observation made her long to disappear, to vanish from his piercing attention, find a place where she could pretend to be invisible. When she began to brood over her situation, she admitted to herself that she had succumbed to the desires of the complacent. Ivan was an esteemably satisfying man, clean as to his person, neat to a fault, marvellously engaged and attentive when they talked or wrestled on the bed, but with him there was no privacy, no hope of any escape to that vacant, windswept plane of tantalising aloneness that Tip longed for.

Disappearance was another matter entirely.

The word usually occurs in a news story containing

the phrase, 'a body believed to be that of…' Anyone could fill in the blank, the cold legal designation summarising human connection, two legs, two arms, dressed in the usual apparel, shoes and watch, carrying a wallet or purse and having spent a bomb on a stylish haircut. Unremarkable but yes, the parts that together comprise discovery.

And the story continues, its phrases rattling toward an inevitable conclusion, 'who disappeared nearly two months ago…found yesterday in a wooded area…' Foul play, that old cheat. Women are often the victims of the foul play refrain. 'Last seen leaving her job at a fish market to pick up her four-year-old son…She never arrived at the nursery.' Followed by the vocabulary of search, policemen slogging through swamp and over vegetative dead-fall, their fluorescent vests marking the ragged line of an exhaustive sweep, determination their bitter motivator. That or a fat reward for sighting the same checked jacket that she was wearing when she left her job. These are the phrases knotted to disappearance, as if it were cousin to criminality, never a matter of choice. The character of disappearance unprepared for, the surprise of the surprise of absence, calls for suspicion.

What about the possibility of concealment, chosen erasure? What about the woman stowing away from an inadequate or just slightly on the verge of not-quite-radish life? What about the woman determined to leave town, wave goodbye, push eject, exit stage right, go up in smoke? What about the woman who vanished without a trace, but by a means of her own devising? In truth, many people who go missing are not victims of foul play, but voluntary vanishers. This Tip knew.

And so she brooded over the notion of vanishing until it came to her one Wednesday morning, her chair aligned neatly in front of her keyboard, her feet side by side on the floor, checking the final figures for the directorate asset register, that she could plan to disappear. She turned the idea over, examining its underside. How can a person disappear? We are traced and tracked, leave behind us such a trail that if those same virtual blips were breadcrumbs, we'd be feeding a flock of raucous birds. But there was surely a way, through the maze of PIN numbers and credit card dockets and hours of security tape to manage to become, if not someone else, at least not yourself.

How to disappear? At first the puzzle was a pleasing distraction for Tip while she organised flow charts and typed lists of applications. She read and listed archetypal stories of disappearance. The man who went down to the pub for a drink. The woman who ducked out for cigarettes or just a breath of fresh air. How they never returned, as if they took a wrong turn, walked down the street into another life entirely. How did they vanish? Their stories persisted as parables of warning: never trust the one who kisses you and says, 'I'll be right back'. Desertion flavoured the recital of disappearing stories. All the sympathy was for the one left behind, wondering at this blow to belief. What drove the deserter to this moment, this abrupt U-turn of commitment, as if living itself were possible to reverse? Tip knew that it need be nothing dramatic, that a fingernail paring could provide sufficient cause.

But searching for a cause was no help to a method.

How did they do it? was Tip's question, and she began to scan the morning papers. How many people disappeared in a year? A thousand? Ten thousand? One hundred thousand, the reports said, in the United States. She could not find statistics for the UK. Most of them children, kidnapped or taken, or women subjected to violence. But wilful disappearance, unusual absence, without explanation? And how long before the survivors gave up looking? Seven years and a person could be declared 'legally dead'. If there was no evidence to the contrary.

Hiding herself tempted Tip. How could she efface every shadow, every trace? Pull a Lord Lucan without the murder and stay quiet as a mouse until the High Court granted probate.

But never were people so measured and recorded. Cameras on the streets, checks and balances on transactions and connections, the tracking maze of telephones and fingerprints. Every breath exhaled evidence. And Tip lived with the reincarnation of Sherlock Holmes, Ivan, priding himself on knowing her motives better than she herself did.

In every life, a moment arrives that says, 'Here is your challenge,' and as time passed, this became Tip's. How could she, an ordinary, easily ignored administrative assistant, vanish? On the days when it seemed she was most invisible to the higher ups she felt her determination solidify. She belonged to that indispensable class, the drones without whom no business could function, but who were always regarded as peripheral, unnecessary. How long would she have to be gone before her being gone was noticed? How much time would she have to cover her tracks? This puzzle cheered Tip. She worked at it when she should have been concentrating on other tasks.

Standing at the back of a meeting room and getting ready to circulate with a plate of orange cheese cubes among priggish-looking salesmen, she wondered what would it take to test their attention. Simple enough. Tip dropped the plate she held. It smashed with amplified heartiness on the slate floor, the cheese bouncing orange dice all around her feet. The district manager actually stopped in the middle of his welcome-to-the-sales-conference speech, looked at her with not reproach but puzzlement, before continuing. She had successfully broken the thread between him and his listeners, though, and they all turned to look, shifting and craning, tittering a bit, as if she were comic relief. She fetched a broom and dustpan, performed the humiliation of clean up, but with an effusive enthusiasm that rattled so much the manager gave up and shooed everyone toward the drinks table. Tip pretended to be embarrassed but she felt secretly vindicated. She had made them notice. They would remember her after she disappeared.

It came to her slowly. The solution was coded in the reverse, the end result. What did investigators who 'found' people look for? If she could know the traces and clues they collected, then she could work backwards and begin to erase those same traces; or even more crucial, make sure to leave none of them. This disappearance would not be a matter of surveillance anyway. That involved watching someone commit unexpected acts. Hers would be a matter of erasure.

But technology is a burr, a bloodhound. If she searched the Internet during tea breaks and lunches, there would be a trace of her search. If she made any inquiries about Social Security Numbers or birth certificates, new credit cards or old identities, there would be some record. The challenge to disappearing was substituting a new identity for the old one without ever actually performing the exchange. Every move had to be cloaked, covert. And preparation was key. She would have to be well provisioned enough to live off the grid of her past, and without making any social agencies suspicious. This became her silent quest, to set herself up so that she could live as someone else, step from her shoes into theirs, a sideways move that left not one tiny strand of hair to incriminate her.

Damn the nosiness of science. Dental records, DNA. There used to be more privacy, no need to worry about investigative procedures digging Q-tips into nostrils, scalpels scraping Achilles heels. Every object that she used or owned now had a serial number and a playback function. She would not be able to drive a car, take a train, or board an aeroplane to escape. She would not be able to access her bank account, her identification would be a liability, and she would need to alter her appearance enough so that she could not be recognised by anyone close to her. Or she would need to find a place on earth that required no identification at all. Disappearance was once easier to carry off. It was common after wars, when de-mobbed men had no home to return to or, shell-shocked and brittle, were unable to remember home. The poor used to be tabulated far less than they are now, and it was no crime to evade census takers. Without the periphrasis of phones and credit cards, it was easy to move along, shift to different parts. Sixty or seventy years ago, people could abandon one worn life and begin another.

In order to conceal her intent, she played contentment. She treated Ivan as if she had settled under the duvet of a mutual future. She laughed at his detective ploys, humoured him even when she found herself grinding her teeth against the urge to make surly retorts to his motive-readings. She still woke at the hour of the wolf, but while she used to gnash her teeth and push boulders uphill, she began to occupy that space between night and dawn by combing her insistent brain for narrow lanes of escape.

'You're happier,' remarked Ivan, one evening when they stopped at the Lamb for a pint.

Tip had to be insouciant. 'Happier?'

'Yes. You frown less. You seem to enjoy the taste of bread and jam.'

Was this pure sarcasm or had he noticed her clenched jaw? Tip gave him a sweet if distracted smile and patted his arm. 'I love your gooseberry jam.'

When he was anxious, Ivan made jam. He did not confess this stress-relieving activity until more than a year after Tip had packed her last box of compact discs and dog-eared paperbacks, closed the door on her tiny flat and handed the key over to the landlord, conspicuously pacing the hallway. The flat was already rented and he needed to slap a coat of paint on the walls, his solution to cleaning. Tip moved in with Ivan, found room for her skirts and jumpers in his closet and in a spurt of tidiness one rainy Saturday began to pull what seemed a huge number of clear glass jars out from a bottom cupboard, a cupboard she thought handy for cereal boxes or canned goods. Ivan came in, dripping, and for the first time, raised his voice.

'What are you doing?'

'Clearing up. I'll re-cycle these.'

'You will not.'

'But they take so much space.'

'I use them.'

'For what?'

He turned his back on her and slowly pulled his arms from the sleeves of his raincoat. 'Jam.'

'Jam?'

'I make jam,' he said. 'When I need to relax.'

Tip sat back on my heels. 'Jam.'

'Yes. Of whatever is in season. Plum. Peach chutney. Marmalade if there is no seasonal fruit to be found.' He hung his coat in the hall and came back into the kitchen looking puffy and defensive, as if to forestall her laughter.

She could not resist. 'Did Sherlock Holmes make jam?'

'Of course not. Look, it relaxes me. The cutting up, the boiling, the pectin to make it set, the colours shining through the glass. Like jewels. And I've noticed you don't mind eating it.'

'You made the jam we've been having? You told me it was your sister's.'

'Actually, those are my efforts.'

She'd caught him in a lie, a small innocuous lie, but a lie nonetheless. Tip scrambled to her feet and flung her arms around his neck. 'I am particularly fond of that pear and ginger combination,' she declared, thinking, at last.

At last.

And so, with a great boiling and bubbling and peeling, sugar sticky on the kitchen floor, the windows steamed with moist heat, Ivan made jam while Tip plotted her escape.

Then came September 11th. Missing people who were grievously missed, who did not want to disappear. Tip felt sick about her own shallow construction, her coward's desire to re-invent a life while others suffered disappearance without volition, the ache of a sudden, shocking void. Such a brutal end to so many contented or coping lives.

But she could not deflect her attention. Were all the missing and presumed dead really both? The truth about such thorough destruction is that it is difficult, no impossible, to identify or count exactly the people killed. The Reported Missing Committee, sieving through fragments and reports and evidence in search of the exact number and identity of the victims, proposed a method and a summary as close to accurate as possible. The dead were named and mourned, but a few people believed to have been killed were found alive and well. In several cases, two names became one person. And discovered too were imaginary names for imaginary people invented by other humans, greedy, scheming humans claiming to have lost loved ones who never existed or who were still alive, living off the grid. That woke Tip up. At such a moment of chaos, fear, unpredictability, a person could walk away and in the confusion of the event, simply disappear. If a person were completely ready, completely calm, willing to wait and plan, for as long as it took to meet the moment when that disappearance was possible. Eight weeks or eight months or eight years. Or longer. But then, to seize, in the ensuing confusion, the opportunity.

Jam or not, she had no interest in insurance fraud. She would not complicate her incognito with furtive crimes, would never claim abduction or memory loss. Which is why she planned her own ambush with absolute and painstaking precision. There might never be an imploded building to effect her imaginary death, but she could be ready when the opportunity presented itself. Ready to become a cipher, a memory, as if she had gotten her hands on an invisibility cloak. Wearing the cloak, viewers could see right through the wearer, as if she were not there. Optical camouflage. But Tip had no access to such wonderful costumes; she had only her wits, sharpened by years of living with Mr Observant Ivan.

Was she not cruel? She feared that she was nothing so wonderfully definite. Like a fever, her cruelty was low-grade, chronic rather than cutting. She wished to re-invent herself, and while some manage to do so by taking up yoga or getting a border collie, she was determined to start over, with a new name and in a new place.

Where would she go? University towns were too youthful, industrial towns too rough-edged. Manchester? Birmingham? Leeds? She was tempted by Leeds. Yorkshire people ask fewer questions than those from the West Midlands. But Tip knew that to be completely safe, she had to leave the UK, find her way to Europe or North America. And since she was a monolingual woman, Europe was less of an option than America. Although everyone she knew dreamed of loitering along the blue waters lapping the Greek islands.

Ivan was not a threatening or hurtful man. Neither abusive nor difficult, he managed only to be boring. Despite his precise observations, his interest in pectin and canning jars, he resonated dullness, inscribed habits and adaptive monogamy. That was, Tip privately acknowledged, her own fault. She had taken up his invitations to the cinema (detective films, of course, where he sat on the edge of his seat as if the clues would be more obvious to an uncomfortable watcher) and to the ritual events sponsored by his firm, Christmas parties and summer picnics. She too had found it useful to invite him along to shadow her less than essential presence at Seaforth events of the same inclination. They settled for one another, and their default congress had now led to this fantasy she worked at with such patient stealth.

Sex? Intimacy between them, despite Ivan's ponderousness, was better than acceptable. He tried harder than most men, slow and fast, holding her astride and above him, or moving gently from behind while she lay like a comma on her side. They managed to enjoy one another, murmur and climax without any screaming pinnacles. Their bodies sighed with satisfaction, but Tip observed that her heart did not threaten to fly from her throat. Still, gentle connection had its own rewards.

Not heartless, she occasionally castigated her own complicity. What a misery she was. She had nothing to complain about. Nothing at all. She did not want to make Ivan unhappy, but if she did not disappear effectively, he would be hunting for clues far longer than he should. On the other hand, she had no wish to leave him under suspicion, the authorities convinced that he had done away with her. Somehow, she would have to ensure his innocence. The fact they had no children was redeeming too. She wouldn't be abandoning a traumatised son or daughter, unable to forget her smell of fragrant moss, her rather stocky legs and strong arms. Idealising the woman that she was not.

Disappearance is more common than we want to believe. Think of all the extinctions, the lost trees and animals, the ships that sank beneath the waters of the sea. Think of Atlantis, the jukebox, dial telephones. Some of these can never be found, some we remember with distant nostalgia, some fade slowly from use. They all disappear, re-cast only through their names, their designations, what they are meant to mean. Tip put herself in the same category, a woman who recognised her own limitations, willing to bow out of the picture.

Ivan would make jam for a month and then, she was convinced, recover. One day, he would find himself walking down the street and set about deducing the reason that the man ahead of him was carrying a package wrapped in brown paper, and what that package contained. He would observe the wrapping, the rectangular satisfaction of the taped ends, and once again record his curiosity with pleasure.

Tip could not prevent anyone from asking the pertinent questions but she could prevent them from discovering the answers. She began to tuck money – crisp, meaningful notes – into a purse she kept on a shelf, a little scuffed but inconspicuous because it was in plain sight. She scanned the death notices every day, looking to find her twin, a woman of her own age and birth date, a possible match. Forged passports and papers could be bought; she needed only the right set of information as a template.

And she linked arms with Ivan, matched his step under their open umbrella. She did not know whether they would ever happen or when, but she waited for those distant explosions to rip open a July day in London.

*

Tip pretends to have erased the faint cave drawings of her past. She thinks she has escaped her recent domesticity. She even believes she has foresworn her seeping, snotty-nosed childhood, but it is engraved on her body, the way she swaggers, the way that her voice comes out patched with rough, the way that she clenches the handles of kitchen knives. Behind the clumsiness that she practises lurks all that she cannot acknowledge.

'Sorry,' she says, and is not.

'Excuse me,' she insists, as if she meant, 'Get out of the way!'

Her speech is a dead give-away. She is, after all, living in a country where she doesn't speak the language, doesn't have a clue about how to say much more than the easy *Hola*, or an authoritative *café con leche, por favor.*

Although she is determined to speak, and with gusto.

'Hola, hola, hola.'

'Café con leche, por favor.'

'Café mediano.'

She'd gotten to Spain easily, the EU route wide open. She can't explain why Spain – certainly not because of any romantic response to mantillas and snorting bulls, and she hasn't a hope of becoming a female bullfighter, not a scant, faint, even remotely accidental hope of reaching for the coloured cape and testing the points of ceremonial swords.

She knows her longings are insidious, unrealistic, even downright romantic, infected by a Hemingwayesque hangover, although she isn't clear who Hemingway was, thinks of him as some big-game fisherman who made a name for himself without intending to reach his own end result, suicide. She headed for Spain because the idea of Spain muttered unintelligible suggestions to her in the thick light of morning, that hour of the wolf again. She imagined she would understand the muttering and understand why she wanted to understand once she got here, as if the country's air will provide a translation.

An imposter she is. No matter where she goes, no matter what colour she dyes her hair or how she holds her shoulders, she can't pass for genuine, the mark that enables invisibility, that makes people step out of the way even while they hold doors open. Tip is her own conundrum, a woman too blaringly present to be ignored and yet too strident to be accepted with gracious courtesy. She can hide, but she cannot camouflage herself enough to drift down a street without heads turning to stare.

Hola, she says gravely to the men who look her square in the face. They do not turn away but regard her judiciously, with the gracious courtesy accorded a suspect. Tip has to laugh. She attracts panhandlers and long-winded pikers who insist on regaling her with their own tortuous childhoods, last weekend's traffic accident or run-in with police. She attracts the attention of those same police, who never stroll past her with politely averted faces, but who look as if they want her to produce a passport and other papers just for walking down the street.

Tip carries a bare minimum of fraudulent identification. No photos, no sentimental connections to family or friends or Ivan or other long lost lovers. Like any impostor, Tip circles these wearying repetitions of visibility, worrying them as if they can provide an answer to her internal revolt and flight, her determined effort to re-invent herself. Divided between what she looks like and what she knows, her body seems to translate the most permeable of sites, an open pit, a scribbled page, a cratered road, a portable economy.

She acquires a large, loose coat to hide her body. She checks her new, illicit passport and her stash of cash, makes sure that her suitcase zippers do not gap and yawn, buys seven pairs of new underwear, those necessary accessories of travel, packing and its restitutions. A woman who has not packed underwear is suspect, traitorous beyond conception. It's a requirement to get through passport control, border crossings, even the outskirts of cities. Tip hates hairdressers, and hates clothing shops even more: one tyrannises her and the other terrorises her. She prefers the thatched friability of her spiky hair, the rough comfort of jeans and cotton t-shirts. Which remind her not to neglect her escape, not to lose the penchant for disappearance that she has worked so hard to perfect. She fingers that asset as palpably as a pebble in her pocket.

Tip knows that to uphold her disappearance she will have to become a good mimic, fade into the background. She has always inhabited an uneasy space, partly tempting, part repulsive. If she were a prostitute, she would be easy to locate, easy to place and to dismiss. But even before her disappearance, she was too slippery for assigned corners. She is a workingwoman, capable of driving and lifting. She types with at least six fingers, and has a hand strong and steady enough to pour tea from industrial pots. She takes orders stoically, doesn't think twice about doing what she's told. It was Ivan's elementary deductions that irked her, forced her to rebel. She smelled, in those long, breathless nights when she found herself sleepless, fermenting socks, unedited armpits, reminders that she was in hiding. But she has not escaped, not yet.

She has made it to Spain, hunkered down in an impossibly out-of-the-way part of the country, a small city sprawled over accordioned hills. Oviedo, in the north, not quite on the sea, not quite near to the boundaries of the Basques or the Saracens, not quite a beautiful, remonstrative city, although it has a few elegant buildings and a densely promenaded park full of pampered, sinewy children who are encouraged to scream at the tops of their lungs.

Tip manages to rent, at an inflated price, a flat in the girdle surrounding downtown, a neighbourhood of nineteenth century blocks and ill-visaged trees, with bulging sidewalks and more than a few pastry shops. Her apartment block is glaringly recent, concocted during the drizzled-out last days of Franco when the very concrete in cement was watered down. Everyone waited for the old dictator to die; even the priests who had supported him rubbed their hands with glee at the roasting he was due for.

An odd space, the flat's triangular layout includes a long kitchen counter, two bedrooms, and no discernible living room, as if life requires only eating and sleeping. Tip knows she has deliberately searched out a place as different from her old London flat as she could find, her bachelor suite cramped as a cat's quarters, but cosy, the bed right in the middle and the kitchen nooked next to the cursory bathroom, although the window sills were exemplary for herbs and potted plants. This one boasts erratic appliances. Tip is wary of the stove and terrified of the washer/dryer combo that neither washes nor dries, merely hisses and thumps and beats clothes around its drum until they are frayed and twisted. Her new underwear looks worn, although she has pulled them up her legs only once. Out the window of the second bedroom is a triangular frame of line, and she pegs her clothes there to air more than to dry, the well of the courtyard booming with the draped flags of every apartment's laundry. If she cranes her neck and looks up, she can see the staggered bunting of sheets and towels and shirts, and even the faint nostalgia of socks.

Her bedroom window opens onto this long vertical airshaft that all the flats share. At night, the cries of lovers and children alike drift into her semi-sleep, invade her elusive dreams.

Darling, my darling.

Sí, sí, sí.

Mama!

She sleeps no better than she did in London, despite having escaped. She has made some progress towards becoming an escapee, but although there is a bullring here, this is not bullfighting country at all. She should have gone farther south, but Tip resists the obvious. Fine to end up in Spain, but she is damned if she'll head for Madrid or Barcelona, where most stories chose to leave adventurous women. Those cities are for escapees who plan outcomes too carefully.

But she takes a lover, a man who drives a delivery truck. He is parked outside her building often enough for the two of them to nod, exchange greetings, and soon enough to drink a *café con leche* together, the preamble to their silently climbing the stairs to Tip's flat, and adding to the cries bouncing between the walls of the air shaft. He has enough English to conduct stark conversations with her, stripped bare, wonderfully lacking in nuance. He owns no ties or elegant jackets, not one, he works in his shirt sleeves. In the heat, his forearms turn the colour of gently simmered creme brulée, while above the sleeve line his skin retains its half-between-white, half-between-brown texture.

Tip, on first touching his exquisite skin, asks him what his background is. 'Hmmm,' she says. 'Where does your family come from?'

'Slovakia,' he tells her, which puzzles Tip. She has insufficient expertise for ethnic comparisons, and besides, she was asking a different question.

'Slovakia?'

'Yes, eastern Europe.'

She cannot explain her query. Where does he *come* from? The same question she asks herself in the middle of the night.

But his skin is so fine that Tip, sleepily stroking the back-and-buttocks length of him, imagines it as a kind of cloth. Not silk, cool and slippery and superior. He is achingly warm, so hot to the touch that sometimes she catches herself snatching her hand away, surprised that she is touching a person and not an iron or a radiator. Nor does his skin resemble cotton with its sturdily milled dependability. He feels like linen carded so fine it has completely lost its stalkiness, become as smooth as the paper that announcements are engraved upon.

Tip's lover takes his skin for granted. He showers and dries himself, dresses without paying even cursory attention to his bossy elbows and his roughened heels. He wears working clothes, pants that are stain resistant, laced boots. He does not have to think himself beautiful because women, and even some men, will do that for him. He merely sets out to begin and then continue and then finish a day, after which he washes the dust from his throat with a beer and tends the rows of radishes and lettuces and carrots that he has planted in a patch behind his mother's house. There are jobs and there are jobs. There are women and there are women, some Spanish, some English, some happy, some sad. The radishes sprout in June.

So Tip tries to rest, lying awake through nights too hot to sleep. She turns and tosses, weighing who she was against who she has become. Short of money, she is reduced to serving again, in a small café at the bottom of her street. The owner, Tonio, is a sweet man who, every morning for a week, brings her orange juice, coffee, and a roll with cheese for breakfast, Tip fumbles out the words for what she wants, and having eaten, scrapes back her chair and stands, ready to roam the city's labyrinthine streets. Trusting, she holds out random coins on her palm so he can take what she owes for the food.

After a week, he asks, his arms circling his body, '*Trabajo?*'

Tip looks at him, shakes her head. She understands so little Spanish that her living here is laughable. How could she imagine she would find any answers? She can't even ask the time or the how to find the nearest bus stop.

'*Trabajo?*'

She shrugs again, her Spanish as invisible as she is not.

He gestures at her, herds her behind the counter and then, with his hands, mimes working the hot steam, the drip coffee filter.

Tip bends to the handle, the coffee scoop, the metal milk pitcher, the old familiar gestures returning as fluidly as remembering to walk. Here is a universal job, one that she has practiced.

The old man beams, then rings open his cash drawer and pulls out a twenty euro note.

'*Trabajo?*' he says.

And Tip nods, so grateful that she smiles. She does not yet need the money, has hoarded enough to keep her for a year. But she has nothing to do, is lonely for routine, a schedule, the need to wake and shower and dress, the need to keep the hours company. And Tonio's glowing, athletic nephews hover around the café, chatting and waiting for their friends.

Tip and the old man work around one another effortlessly, bending and rattling crockery, slicing lemons, and pouring out the slick dregs of coffee, although the only words they exchange are the drinks they serve, the coins they collect.

Café con leche.

Café mediano.

Zumo de naranja.

Too late, Tip discovers that Tonio has a plate-ugly wife who hates Tip on sight. She comes after eleven and every day scolds the old man as if to discredit Tip, pointing at her as if she is a thief and a monster. Tip ignores the decibels but cannot ignore the tone. Her heart goes cold, and she thinks of reaching out and slapping the woman's face but she knows that if she even smiles an eyelash too far, she will be locked out, the old woman will emerge from the tiled back room where she shoves thinly-sliced ham and cheese into the yeasty cheeks of fresh rolls, and run her off with a broom, her arms waving, her own cheeks puffed with scorn.

Tip came to Spain as a refugee from herself. She is not able to open her mouth and speak Spanish. She listens to the noise of the arguments that echo in the courtyard without knowing their meaning, tries to decipher tone in their vibration. She foams milk and drinks coffee and takes her lover up the stairs. Her lover pulls all the radishes. The old man worries that the coffee machine will splutter to death, and Tip watches the street passing outside the window and thinks about renting a car, or driving toward the high plains of the interior where the black shadows of the sherry-bulls loom in stark relief, as if to challenge clichés. None of them can imagine who they are or what life they will inhabit or when, like Tonio's wife, they are old and almost ugly. Tip sleeps and tosses and wakes at the hour of the wolf, missing the past that she has renounced. Each day she climbs the stairs to her flat as exhausted as if she has fought a battle. She opens the window onto the airshaft, the shriek of the laundry pulleys and the calls of children home from their school afternoons threading into her room.

And surprises herself, one day, by asking Tonio for a week off. Not surprising that she asks him for time off, but that she manages so easily to make her request known, manages to let him know in reasonably intelligible Spanish that she needs a reprieve from the hiss of the steam and the push of elegant customers through the glass door.

She doesn't go far, just an hour away, to the coastal

town of Cudillerro, its pastel houses and staggered progress up the steep cliff behind the harbour a living ladder. She makes herself lazy, leaves her room no earlier than eleven. In the cafés of the town square she watches the feral cats fight over fish bones, watches German tourists point their cameras at the austere church. She climbs the zigzag steps to the graveyard and lies on a polished death stone, napping in the sea breeze curling off the Atlantic. The protesting bones of the dead murmur beneath her, and then she wakes and wanders down the cliff again, to feast on the salty lick of barbequed sardines caught fresh from the sea.

From across the slate-coloured waves, she feels the pull of North America, the new world through the portal of Halifax with its history of welcoming boats and immigrants and emigrants and lost souls in search of a shore and a reinvented self. Is it possible to disappear again, over there? And if it is possible, is it easier or harder? What a question, what a question to ask herself in the Spanish of Spain. Tip shivers in the heat. She skirts the curved womb of Cudillerro's sheltered harbour and decides that she will have to try to reconcile her history with her disappearing fiction.

Leave, she whispers to herself. Leave. It's time to go. Invent yourself again. She sits down at a table by the harbour and orders a drink, turning the glass around and around in her hand. A group of elegant Spanish women, perfect in appearance, take over the patio. They order vermouth, and drink in unison, their glasses clicking their teeth. Through their babble, Tip envisions herself an eternal impostor, a monster split between two completely different worlds. The blessing/curse, she thought, is that one can never escape the other.

She returns to her lover's city, the innocence of Oviedo, accomplice to her flight. The next morning she walks into the café and serves coffee as patiently as an anchorite. Tonio looks at her and frames a question, but she shrugs, although she understands that he is concerned, thinks her unwell. At two, siesta time, remembering again the texture of her lover's skin, she wanders down the street in search of a telephone and manages to call him. He does not answer the phone. She goes up to her flat and takes a siesta alone. That is the right thing to do in the heat of the afternoon. She does not know how to rescue her body from its flight, but she falls across the bed and sleeps as she had not managed to sleep since she arrived. And then she dreams of Canada.

*

At the back door, behind the grey hulk of the cinder-block factory, in the buzzing light of an overhead post, Tip leans against the wall, taking deep breaths and thinking about the west. Western Canada. Saskatchewan. Alberta. Ranch hands and rodeos. Big clouds. She is not really trapped in Scarborough, in a sweeping hatchery of low-browed buildings. She is camping in Banff National Park, lolling in the mineral pool, bobbing through the hot sulphur water and smelling the piney smell of mountain trees.

She came out to quell her nausea, her sudden knowledge that she would throw up, the smell more than she can bear. She has been breathing quick shallow breaths all evening, fighting the chemical stench of the material that they coat the boxes with.

The door grinds open behind her and Graham shoulders out, his over-sized hockey moustache quivering.

'Hey, you all right?'

'Whew.'

'Rory's looking. Told him you just went to piss.'

'Jesus,' says Tip. 'Do we need a union or what. One minute and the floor boss is asking where I am.'

'Take it easy.'

'Take it easy! We're being asphyxiated in there, and the floor boss wants to know why we don't just stay and enjoy it.'

'Wear a mask.'

'Makes it worse and you know it, Graham. Those stupid little mesh things just trap the smell.'

'You pregnant?'

'Please.'

'Okay, just asking, but we'd better get back.'

'All right, be right there.'

Tip tilts her head and takes a long look at the sky, a sky that she remembers looking at so carelessly, here as murky as soup, humid in summer and in winter dank and cold.

The box factory is exactly that, a factory that makes boxes, that pounds and compresses woodchips into cardboard and corrugated cardboard, that shapes and presses the cardboard into large sheets, which are cut and stamped into the incipient shapes of boxes. The boxes are never finished, their squares and rectangles filled with air, but are left flat, stacked and then tied together. If only there were boxes, Lego blocks containing something, even shredded cardboard itself, but these boxes are all ideas, threatening with their lack of geometry.

Tip works the huge cutter that punches out the lines that enable the cardboard to be bent and folded so that the slits become the openings, the tabs that close over the open ends. The machine is like a massive punch, hydraulic, and all she has to do is pull a lever for ten cardboard sheets to be forced into the form of potential boxes. The job isn't bad, she needs to be dextrous more than strong, but tonight they are making boxes coated with some kind of bug-proof or waterproof stuff, and the floor stinks of chemicals, a particularly vivid bleach and moth-ball combination that makes their eyes water and their noses bleed.

She wants to walk off, just quit, but then how will she pay for the cramped rooms she rents in the basement of the walk-up? She just, at this stage, needs enough money to hit the road again. She will do anything to go west, get out of this hot, heartless swamp in central Canada. She expected Toronto to be small, homey, with painted porches and lots of pine trees. 'Toronto,' she declares to the immigration agent. 'I'm staying in Toronto.' She feels as if she should be smoking a cigarette while she says that, should be sporting fashionable shoes and a bouffant hair-do.

Toronto. Well, this isn't Toronto, but then it is Toronto. It is Scarborough, Toronto's armpit, and so far, she hasn't seen much that isn't Toronto's armpit. Toronto, Tip rapidly decides, is all armpit, unless you are a baseball fan or hustle a regular invitation to dinner with one of the artsy people in literature or music. But that will not happen to Tip. She hitches herself back to the console of her machine, pulls the hydraulic lever down and hisses out a stack of box forms that look like over-sized puzzle cookies. She gestures for the fork to lift those away and another stack to descend, and she pulls the hydraulic lever down and hisses out another stack of boxes that look like over-sized puzzle cookies. She blinks to try and ease the burning behind her eyes, and she pulls the hydraulic lever down and hisses out a stack of boxes that look like over-sized puzzle cookies.

'Come on, Tip,' she says out loud. Come on. Sixty-eight more pulls of the lever until four am, coffee break time. The coffee is terrible and the coffee room smells like the rest of the factory. No escape there, or from the nude pin-ups or the men playing poker. Sixty-eight more pulls after that and she can pick up her lunch bucket and punch out, walk nine blocks to a bus stop, wait for a diesel-foul bus, and then ride forty-two minutes to get home.

Home. She doesn't even have the best kind of landlord, a pushover. This job isn't as bad as being the magician's apprentice. It is worse, far worse. She would rather be sawn in half six times a night, she would rather stand there with that goofy handkerchief and the dove shitting down her arm, she would rather lie on the floor and be walked on. She gestures for the fork to lift the stack of cardboard away and another stack to descend, and she pulls the hydraulic lever down and hisses out a stack of box-shapes that look like over-sized puzzle cookies.

When the lift picks these up, the operator jerks the fork and the stack falls, not yet strapped together with those powerful little plastic sashes that snap around the middle. The box forms tumble to the floor, twelve awkward shapes that need to be gathered and straightened, that, if they were sheets of paper, could be picked up by hand and neatly adjusted. But these are as big as Tip herself is, and the operator will have to wrestle them together.

'Shit.' He doesn't really scream but grunts, grinds the forklift to a stop. 'SHIT.'

'Watch your language.'

'Up yours, honey.'

'And yours too.' These are cheerful insults, necessary for the flow of work, and they mean nothing, are like saying, 'Too bad,' or 'Hey, I'm sorry.' This is the language that workers pace themselves through, the flow of their own impetus.

He bends over the boxes, trying to push them together, yelling, 'Hey, somebody want to give me a hand here?' when the forklift—he must not have set the brake, or its very vibration has set it in motion – begins to creep toward him.

'Hey,' Tip shouts – and he looks up toward her for a startled moment, as if to interrupt himself, this is not a friendly exchange but a warning – and she waves, 'Get out the way. Look out!'

He looks past her as if the danger comes from that direction, then turns – and yes, it is as slow as choreography – towards the lift's arms moving as if to nudge him or pull him close. And without him or Tip even gesturing another move or uttering another syllable, the forklift, an effortless and benign cyborg, tantalisingly gentle, pushes him to the ground. He scrambles back and Tip has already ground her hydraulic to a halt, is racing toward the machine, its motion ungainly but taking hours to reach, those few minutes like molasses, she tries to get her foot onto the platform, grabbing at anything to pull herself up, get her hand on the gear, the off switch, throwing it and tearing at the brake, then running for the wall and pressing the emergency button. It wails to life while she turns to Lecker on the floor, no blood, but his writhing body, his not screaming, that is the worst, the worst. The whole floor comes running, all the machines halted in mid-gasp, the smell still stinging, everywhere the smell, and Tip thinks, that's why our reflexes are slower, the smell, and the floor boss gets there first, the bastard, hasn't called first aid or emergency, and Tip runs for the telephone—the only one – on the wall, punches 911 and gets that nasal Ontario voice that she suddenly realises she hates with a hatred shocking even to her, at this moment, in this situation.

'I hate you,' she says into the phone, and the voice on the other end, female, says, 'Calm down. Give me your location, fine yes, the ambulance is on the way,' without even responding to Tip's initial statement.

The floor boss is pulling at Lecker, as if getting him on his feet will prove that nothing has happened, but the rest are saying to leave him alone, get a blanket, and the first aid men come – 'I've called 911, they're on their way,' shouts Tip – their portable stretcher not much more than a plank and lift Lecker's sagging body onto the plank and stagger with him away to the lunch room.

'Okay, okay,' Rory looks around at their faces, suddenly blanched, the machines hissing as they wait. 'Back to work.'

'Hey, no Worker's Comp investigation?'

'We don't even know if he's hurt.'

'We don't even know if he's hurt,' she mimics. 'He's lying on the floor looking like grey dog shit and we don't even know if he's hurt. Hey, there's no blood, it must be internal, that's not bad.'

'Shut up and get back to work.'

Tip folds her arms across her chest. 'Maybe, if you turn the ventilation on. Maybe, if you let us find out how Lecker is.'

'You know fucking well the ventilation's automatic. And Lecker's okay.'

'Yeah, the fans go on for three minutes an hour just to make sure they don't use too much electricity.'

They are all staring at her as if they haven't seen her before, and in truth, they haven't, one set of hands as good as another's, and the ventilation is bad, and poor fucking Lecker, he'll be fired if he's not damaged, and they've never had any loyalty to Rory, he's a pig, never easing up for even a moment, and so they all fold their arms across their chests just like she does and stand there.

There's no dramatic confrontation. No fighting, that would be too western. Rory just turns and stomps away, and they stand in a version of circle while the ambulance arrives and while he supervises Lecker being moved more professionally now by white-jacketed men who speak in low, comforting voices and move with padded swiftness. Rory goes with them, as if he is in charge.

And it is Tip who bends to the scattered, punched-out box shapes and pulls one erect and, holding the thick flat cardboard against her body as if it were a dance-partner, begins to fold the stamped cardboard into a box that will define space. She spreads the sides together so that it stands on end, then does the bottom flaps, working around the box which is as tall as she is, then, pulls over a step-ladder so that she can finally close the top flaps. Standing there, in the middle of the floor, is what they make, the shape that will enclose some real object.

Although it is still a box full of nothing. Boxes of cardboard, empty, ready to become receptacles, to hold food or clothing or parts or even air, shipping containers for the rest of the country, sent from the centre, radiating out towards the sweet-smelling edges of Canada. Tip can see in her mind this waterproofed and heavy-duty cardboard box travelling toward the west, holding some trendy gear for humid weather that sure the hell Alberta doesn't need, and on the floor again, she kicks at a corner so the box shifts. After all, it is empty.

She walks around it, looking at the perfect corners, the mathematically measurable eloquence of its shape, and decides right then and there, that she is going west. Disappearing again.

*

Voyeurs want disappearance to improve occasion, recite a lesson, manhandle a moral. Oh yes, he was asking for it, she was certainly on the wrong track, and now we can relegate her to the back of the shoe bin, the box collecting stuff that nobody wants anymore. Just desserts is what attracts eavesdroppers, the ones who want to control the outcome of every destination, make the missing live up to their obligations, pay their bills, dust the dusty shelves. Don't forget to charge them double, serves them right to be sent to the longest line in the passport office, and do you have your documentation in triplicate? No further details available.

Vanishing is a threat that hovers like a high wall, bland and endless. It can only cause embarrassment, like a friend who admits to extra-terrestrial sightings, ghosts in the basement. Discomfited, everyone wants to change the subject. And the disappeared don't wait around to be announced as such, don't offer famous last words, the closing grace notes of the non-obituary. No body, no notice. Hometown reviews of the last seen usually talk about whether they liked ice cream or the hobbies they used as revenge. Model trains, big band songs, a rock collection.

Corn, beans, squash. Taste can be forgotten too, become old-fashioned and obsolete, like dial telephones and cash registers that grind toward a total, like the return bell on typewriters and Toni at-home perms.

Absence has a shape as detailed as a presence. Human chronologies assemble around an empty place to form a silhouette, an ambuscade. In that cosy void, features chime recognisable as the faces of old friends or persistent enemies.

Here is the truth. Despite the detailed numbers that are kept, there is no registry of the whereabouts of the bodies of the living and the imagined dead, no institutional record, no memory in charge of the drowning faked for insurance, the man who vanished while swimming along the shore. Nothing left behind except his shoes, aggrieved and loose, the tongues lolling under the laces.

Here is advice. Remember to register your cell phone under an alternate name. Time your disappearance with your double. A truck driver is certain to remember that he caught a glimpse of you, the missing person, by the side of the road. The tired cabdriver will remember that he dropped you right in front of the house. Adults cannot disappear.

Reported missing on Tuesday, she turned up Thursday two weeks later. Vanish if you can, but if you can't pull it off, then get yourself 'found' in good condition and claim amnesia. *Entre nous,* you know that they'll be watching you once you want to disappear. Before that, they don't bother.

And don't resist the best of the *en tapinous,* the ultimate camouflage. On sale now. Put one on to disappear from view, get out of tight scrapes. Your very own invisibility cloak, a garment that makes it possible to see straight through the wearer. They call it emerging technology, this optical illusion, augmented reality. Scientists declare it made of 'retro-reflective material,' covered with light-reflective beads. The designer versions have cameras that project what is at the back of the wearer onto the front to make the wearer blend into her background. Double indemnity. Optical camouflage. But you know better. Despite the wave of the wizard, the computer in the cloak a cosy machine, this is an artificial disappearance, mechanical. It's useful only for aggressive action, voyeurism. Cloaks do not make the stowaway. Real disappearance is a matter of incognito, eclipse.

Pity those left behind, those who try to trail the ones who've vanished, those left wondering. Listen to their stories and give them the comfort of the well-conducted search.

But never pity those who disappear by choice.

The Authors

'The Last Night' by Storm Jameson (© Storm Jameson 1943) is reproduced by kind permission of PFD (www.pfd.co.uk) on behlf of the estate of Storm Jameson.

'A Love Song For Miss Lillian' by Mark McWatt is published in *Suspended Sentences*, Peepal Tree Press, Leeds. www.peepaltreepress.com

Storm Jameson was born in Whitby in 1891, a prolific novelist and activist she is best known for her inter-war trilogy *Mirror In Darkness* and her autobiography *Journey From The North*. She died in 1986. **Mark McWatt** was born in Guyana, studied in Canada and Leeds and now teaches in Barbados. Best known as a poet his collection of stories *Suspended Sentences* won the Commonwealth Prize for Best First Book, and is published by Peepal Tree Press in Leeds. **Patricia Duncker** has published two collections of stories and four novels, *Hallucinating Foucault* won her the Dillons First Fiction Award. Professor of Creative Writing at UEA she is Visiting Professor for Yorkshire's development programme for young writers, The Writing Squad. **Artitha van Herk** has published five novels, as well as two works of non-fiction, *In Visible Ink* and *A Frozen Tongue* which explore elements of silence and seduction. Her most recent expedition into time and words is *Mavericks: An Incorrigible History of Alberta*, which won the Grant McEwan Author's Award.

For more biography and background on all the Light Transports writers go to **www.light-transports.net**

Ideas Above Our Station

ISBN 1 901927 28 8

Price £8.99

Someone is waiting for a train, or it could be a bus or an aeroplane. They are alone. For company, in their coat pocket they are carrying a book of stories. They sit down and take out the book. It falls open on the first page of a new story. What would be the perfect read for them to find there?

Fifteen writers have risen to the challenge to put the ideal story into their fellow traveller's hand. The results are inside this book.

Ideas Above Our Station is a title in the acclaimed Route series of contemporary stories.

'Sharp, refreshing and full of surprises...a bit like going to a party and meeting one fascinating person after another.'

'Route is a trailblazing publisher of literary talent. Here you'll find some of the best short storytelling since Raymond Carver.'

For details of this book and our full books programme, including the new downloadable byteback books, please visit

www.route-online.com

Light Transports

Light Transports is a series of three books, distributed free at train stations across Yorkshire in October 2006 as part of the Illuminate Festival. Each book is filled with stories appropriate for different journey lengths; *A Couple Of Stops*, *Commutes* and *Intercity*.

A Couple Of Stops
ISBN 1 901927 29 6
Featuring stories from Winifred Holtby, Tom Spanbauer, Mandy Sutter, Steven Hall, Ellen Osborne, Chenjerai Hove and Kath McKay.

Commutes
ISBN 1901927 30 X
Featuring stories from Alecia McKenzie, MY Alam, Jack Mapanje and Sumeia Ali.

Intercity
ISBN 1901927 31 8
Featuring stories from Storm Jameson, Mark McWatt, Patricia Duncker and Aritha van Herk.

For more details visit www.light-transports.net

**For more books from Route
visit www.route-online.com**